Praise for
SHERI REYNOLDS

"Ms. Reynolds's poetic gifts are uncommonly powerful."
—*The New York Times*

"Reynolds is a wonderful storyteller and master of pastoral imagery."
—*The New York Times Book Review*

"Reynolds . . . is a gifted writer with a deceptively simple style and a keen ear for dialogue." —*The Boston Globe*

"Reynolds is the newest and most exciting voice to emerge in contemporary southern fiction." —*San Francisco Bay Guardian*

"*The Rapture of Canaan* is a book about miracles, and in writing it, Reynolds has performed something of a miracle herself."
—Oprah Book Club selection review

"[A]s true as butter in your grits. . . . [a] powerful drama with pathos, poetry, and, unexpectedly, hope."
—*People* magazine, for *The Sweet In-Between*

"[A] sweet coming-of-age story, thanks to its young, wise-beyond-her-years, Scout Finch-esque heroine."
—*Entertainment Weekly,* for *The Sweet In-Between*

the HOMESPUN WISDOM of MYRTLE T. CRIBB

SHERI REYNOLDS

TURNER

Turner Publishing Company

200 4th Avenue North • Suite 950
Nashville, Tennessee 37219

445 Park Avenue • 9th Floor
New York, NY 10022

www.turnerpublishing.com

The Homespun Wisdom of Myrtle T. Cribb

Copyright © 2012 Sheri Reynolds. All rights reserved.
This book or any part thereof may not be reproduced or transmitted in any form
or by any means, electronic or mechanical, including photocopying, recording, or
by any information storage and retrieval system, without permission in writing
from the publisher.

Cover design by Gina Binkley
Book design by Glen M. Edelstein
Cover illustrations by Giselle Potter

Library of Congress Cataloging-in-Publication Data

Reynolds, Sheri.
  The homespun wisdom of Myrtle T. Cribb / Sheri Reynolds.
    p. cm.
  ISBN 978-1-61858-013-9
  1.   Special education educators--Eastern Shore (Md. and Va.)--Fiction. 2.
Dysfunctional families--Fiction. 3. Marital conflict--Fiction. 4. Man-woman
relationships--Fiction. 5. Friendship--Fiction. I. Title.
  PS3568.E8975H66 2012
  813'.54--dc23
                              2012014188

Printed in the United States of America
12 13 14 15 16 17 18—0 9 8 7 6 5 4 3 2 1

For Sammie Cannon Jordan

ACKNOWLEDGMENTS

With thanks and love to my readers and advisors: Barbara Brown, Christin Lore Weber, Amy Tudor, Candice Fuhrman, Shaye Areheart, Jenean Hall, Ned Brinkley, Andrew Follmer, Patsy Reynolds, Sammie Jordan, Caroline Blanton, Alexis Jordan, and Mary Beth Byrd.

And with much appreciation to my new publishing team: Marcy Posner, Diane Gedymin, and Christina Huffines.

FOREWORD

Just down the road from my house, there's the cutest little bungalow you ever imagined. For many years, it had four wisteria trees growing out front. Every spring the owner pruned and shaped those trees, until the ropey trunks thickened and the tops filled in, lush and green, vine-tentacles sprawling. Those trees looked like they wanted to hug each other—like they were reaching out to hug everybody that passed by. You couldn't help feeling happy when you saw them.

Then one day the owner choked on a lamb chop and died. The house sold, and the new owners hacked those amazing trees to the ground. They didn't even do a good job of it, sawing haphazardly, wrenching and twisting off what was left. It looked like a wisteria slaughtering, and I cried about it for half an hour (which was only seven and a half minutes per tree, if you divvy it up, and certainly they deserved more than that). I called my best friend, Dottie, and told her to drive by and see what those new owners had done, and later that morning she called back and said, "Well, thank the Lord. Now you can finally see that gorgeous house!"

For most of my life, I thought the way I saw the world was the right and reasonable way, and I tried to convince anybody who saw it differently to come over to my side. Then I had an experience that exploded my thinking and opened me to possibilities I couldn't have dreamed. Now it's all I can do not to shout my story from the street corner—and I would except that our little town doesn't even have a red light, so there's no sufficient place for me to preach it. Instead I've written this book to share what I've learned, in the hopes that it might make your life a little bit better, too.

But before I go on, a disclaimer: I'm not a spiritual teacher in any traditional sense. Unlike many enlightened souls, I can't claim to have heard the voice of God whispering from the cornfields, and the only time an angel beckoned to me in a dream, she spoke in voodoo gibberish. Unlike many transformed souls, I've never experienced a psychotic break, though, as my husband Craig will tell you, I've thrown a glass of wine against a wall and seen miraculous images in the purple splatters left behind on tests I'd been correcting. I've never distinguished myself at formal meditation, and after I turned forty, my thighs got too chunky to hold the lotus position for long. When I light a candle, take a deep breath, and concentrate on the flame, my mind turns not to God, but to enchiladas, and I end up at Don Fernando's again, eating too many greasy chips with fire sauce. I've heard of spiritual teachers who entered psychiatric facilities wearing nothing but their fuzzy bedroom slippers. Years later, on national TV, they speak in calm, enlightened tones of how right-breathing brings peacefulness. Always their hair is soft and wavy, their yoga britches perfectly black.

I'm not that kind of guide.

Nor am I particularly religious, though I helped with Vacation Bible School when I was a younger woman and sang in the choir before the choir director quit and the sopranos ran amuck. The only vows I've taken have been the obvious ones, and those I made quite stupidly, as most young people do. I'm not the sort of spiritual teacher who earned my insights through contemplation or in a cloister.

What I am is a middle-aged white woman from the Eastern Shore of Virginia who took a road trip—an accidental pilgrimage—with a black man many people would label a vagrant and a bum. That experience changed and deepened me, transforming my life, my marriage, and my relationships with others. In the year since my journey, I've set down on record the events in the form of this devotional for ordinary folks in the hopes that some of what I experienced might help you with your own journey. For yes, you *are* on a journey, even if you don't know it yet.

In my story you'll find insights I've gleaned from my experiences, but also tidbits I've picked up from self-help books and sermons, from speakers at spiritual retreats, and at conferences for educators. I've even learned that certain refrigerator magnets can bring you closer to the Divine, and when applicable, I refer to those, too.

Feel free to read this book in whatever way works best. You can place it near your Bible by your bedside table, or you can leave it on your back porch or in your powder room. You can experience it once a day, a section at a time, or you can read it all at once and come back later to do the Activities for Further Growth. No matter how you choose to use this book, it's my great hope that my simple story will help you in some profound way.

Wishing you blessings and a peaceful heart —

Myrtle T. Cribb

CLARKE
LOUDOUN
Moorefield
HARDY
GRANT
Petersburg
WARREN
Front Royal
SHENANDOAH
Woodstock
FAUQUIER
PRINCE
Manassas
Warrenton
PAGE
Franklin
ROCKINGHAM
MADISON
Culpeper
Harrisonburg
Madison
Stanardsville
GREENE
Orange
ORANGE
SPOTSYLVANIA
AUGUSTA
Charlottesville
Louisa
Staunton
Waynesboro
LOUISA
ALBEMARLE
Palmyra
FLUVANNA
GOOCHLAND
NELSON
Lovingston
Lexington
Goochland
POWHATAN
AMHERST
BUCKINGHAM
Powhatan
CUMBERLAND
Amherst
Buckingham
Cumberland
Amelia CH
APPOMATTOX
Lynchburg
AMELIA
Bedford
Appomattox
Rustburg
Farmville
PRINCE EDWARD
NOTTOWAY
CAMPBELL
Charlotte CH
CHARLOTTE
Lunenburg
LUNENBURG
Lawrenceville
Chatham
HALIFAX
MECKLENBURG
PITTSYLVANIA
Halifax
Boydton

PART ONE

1

What I did was no more interesting or sinful than this: I took a handful of my husband, Craig's, back pain pills with me when I left that morning for my little operation because I was worried about the potential for pain later in the day. I worried that the doctor might tell me to take ibuprofen—because male doctors often do that to females, refuse to prescribe for them what they'd automatically prescribe for a man; some of them don't even realize they're still blaming Eve—and I didn't want to suffer on my drive back home or into the night. So I took a handful of Craig's medicine as a simple precaution.

My nerves were kinked and frazzled. I'd been up most of the night worrying, and to complicate things more, the fog that morning was so thick you couldn't see, the kind of fog we refer to around here as a malignancy of air. My side mirrors were clouded and wet, and my rearview mirror was broken, so I could barely see to back out of the driveway. Back then I drove Craig's old green truck with the camper top on it. The rearview mirror had been gone for so long that when Craig had taken the truck in for its yearly inspection, he'd had to bribe the fellow to give us a sticker with some fresh flounder he'd caught that day. So, backing out of the driveway, I rolled down the window, stuck my head out as best as I could, and said a prayer that anything with sense enough to hear the tires crunching on the crushed up clam shells would stay out of my way.

Fog can confuse you because everything looks like an x-ray of itself, recognizable but not reliably so. As I made my way up the road, I gripped the wheel harder than I needed to, feeling not quite like myself. I worried about Craig out there on his boat. The crabbing season had just started up, but how would they even be able to find their crab pots in that weather? Depending on visibility, he might have to come back in, or maybe he was still in the harbor, waiting out the fog. And wouldn't it be just my luck if he decided to swing by the school to bring me flowers (something he's never done) and discover that I'd taken off for the doctor's appointment I'd kept a secret from him?

So I was anxious, naturally, and I caught myself gulping air by accident. I didn't want to have gas by the time I got to the doctor, especially considering the region of my body where he'd be working. That's when I decided to take one of Craig's pain pills—to relax my muscles and calm my nerves, offsetting any potential pain, and also, hopefully, preventing the pootsies.

I don't know if you can blame the drugs for what happened next. My appointment was a two-hour drive away, scheduled for eleven, so I had plenty of time to think. But as I got closer to the doctor's office, the truck started slowing down. It seemed like my foot didn't have the power to push that gas pedal hard enough to get me there on time. I started second-guessing myself, thinking that if I was going to spend my entire secret savings, it should be on something I looked forward to, maybe a trip with my girlfriend Dottie to Atlantic City to play the slot machines or to Pigeon Forge, Tennessee, where Dolly Parton sings.

With Craig's medicine in me, loosening me up, I started wondering if I should be getting my procedure done at all. It was elective surgery and wouldn't have been covered by my insurance even if I'd been fool enough to show them my benefits card. Of course, then the Human Resources supervisor at the elementary school where I work might find out what Craig had been teasing me about for years: I'm lopsided down there, between my legs, with one regular-sized lip and the other one pouting over it. Craig used to make jokes. Sometimes he'd accuse me of attempting to sprout a little ding-a-ling of my own. Sometimes when I'd get out of the shower, he'd point and laugh until I hopped into my panties. "For Lord's sake, baby," he'd say. "Can't you roll that thing up and tuck it somewhere?"

Now where was I supposed to tuck it?

(If it makes you squirm to read this, take a deep breath and hang in there. There are women all over creation ashamed of their bodies, and we need to talk about it more than we do.)

To his credit, Craig always ended such conversations saying things like, "I'm just messing with you, baby. Don't sulk," or else he'd bring me home a milkshake to make up. But I lived with that kind of teasing day in and day out, and ultimately, it was what drove me toward my spiritual awakening. Right there on that highway headed north, I got just as gnarly-hearted as I could be. What right did Craig have to make me feel bad about my biology? I didn't pick my coochie size any more than I picked my eye color. I got mad with that doctor who'd sworn I'd be happier when I was *symmetrical*, showing me pictures of other women who looked like little girls and making me think I wanted to look that way, too.

And I got aggravated with myself for being suckered by them both. I got so mad that when I stopped to fill up the gas tank, I bought myself a Slurpee—a big one (I wasn't supposed to have anything to eat or drink before my procedure), and I took *another* one of those pills, this time *just because I could.*

I drove right past that doctor's office, blowing the horn and shooting the bird at somebody in the parking lot. (That's not something I'm proud of, and I only tell you this to demonstrate the degree of my frustration. That poor woman was probably there to have her clitoris dehooded, bless her bones.) At that point, I didn't know where I was headed. I just knew that wherever it was, I was going to have my oversized lippy when I got there.

So these were the conditions that led me to the place where I am today, and here are some things to consider, if you ever find yourself in similar straits.

MEATY TIDBITS

Your body isn't a topiary garden. There's nothing wrong with one body part being shaped differently than another. If your husband, wife, or otherwise beloved gives you grief about your symmetry, send that person out into the natural world. Look at the trees growing in your yard or neighborhood. Trees don't grow symmetrically. They stretch and branch and sometimes even contort themselves. The only trees and bushes that look perfectly symmetrical are owned by neurotics with hedge trimmers. These people are akin to plastic surgeons, and you'd do well to stay away from them.

If trees and plants aren't proof enough, have a look at the birds. Go sit on your porch and watch the little finches that make nests in your hanging fern and keep you from being able to take it down when it dies. If you can get a finch to stop hopping around long enough, you'll see that the feathers on either side don't match precisely. Watch the cat, sitting on the mailbox, hoping to grab the finch right out of the fern. The cat has one black paw when all the rest are tabby, and do you think that cat goes around ruminating and bellyaching about it? The cat knows it's perfect as it is. You're also perfect. So before you go looking for someone to balance your breasts, before you wear your hair in a strange configuration to hide your over-large ears, just remember: you could have bigger problems. You could be a finch with asymmetrical feathers, living in a half-dead fern, stalked by a cat with mismatched paws who won't give a fe-fi-fo-fum about your feathers when he crunches down on your tiny bones. Symmetry is overrated. Think about that before you go lopping off your own meaty tidbits.

2

I can't tell you exactly how many miles I'd traveled when I heard something knocking around under my truck. At first I thought I'd run over a stick, and it'd hung up on my axle and was whacking against the asphalt. But the knocking became more insistent, and then it seemed to be coming from behind me. When I turned around, what I saw scared the devil right out of me and set in motion the next stage of my journey. For there, in the back of my hand-me-down Dodge pickup, was Hellcat—stowed-away, pounding at the camper-top glass with both fists and staring at me with his bugged-out, bloodshot eyes.

Naturally, I ran off the road, swerving into a shallow ditch and bumping out the other side. I hit the brakes and skidded, but didn't stop until my bumper'd grazed the sign outside the First Methodist Church of Lambs and Lions. As soon as I could catch my breath, I looked into the back again where Hellcat crawled around, trying to steady himself. I'd sent him tumbling when I wrecked.

I got to the tailgate as Hellcat was pushing open the camper top, but before I could ask him what he was doing, he'd leaped out, gagging, and run over to some bushes. Through his vomiting and choking, he kept calling out, "Wait for me, now!" and "Don't you leave me here!"

It's no exaggeration to say that I was distressed. Immediately

I thought about Craig and what he'd do. When he found out about Hellcat and saw that I'd wrecked the truck, he'd have a stroke. He'd forget all about the fog that morning, the low visibility, the fact that I couldn't have known Hellcat was back there because I couldn't see a thing. I found Hellcat's rake in the truck bed and used it to pull out a dozen crumpled up Colt 45 cans, along with the sleeping bag I kept with me in case of emergencies. Evidently, Hellcat had passed out drunk on it. From the smell, I couldn't tell if he'd peed there or spilled some of his malt liquor.

When he staggered out of the bushes, he looked like something dragged back from the grave, gleaming with sweat, lips swollen and glazed. He wiped his thick hand across his mouth and muttered, "Where we at?"

I couldn't tell him exactly. "I've driven a right good ways," I admitted, and he nodded and said he was dizzy and climbed back into the truck. I gave him the smelly sleeping bag to cover up with, and we bumped back onto the road. The truck drove fine, but poo! My nerves! I had to take another pill then. I needed to calm down just to figure out what to do next.

You have to understand the gravity of my situation: Hellcat was the town vagrant. A tall, lanky black man with prominent freckles and an uneven reddish afro, perpetually filthy clothes, and a limp, he dragged himself everywhere he went. He was always asking for odd jobs, wanting to rake your leaves for five dollars or ten, depending on the size of your yard. Or he'd walk down the street lugging an old broken lamp, the electric cord dragging behind him, and he'd try to sell it to you for a dollar or two, enough money to buy a bottle of liquor. He slept wherever he found a quiet place—in abandoned buildings or construction sites. One time Craig found him sleeping on a pile of dried out eel grass in a shack behind the harbor where they used to keep the crab floats. Apparently he'd picked my truck as his latest bedroom.

Maybe he'd slept in my truck a hundred times and gotten out early, before I left for work. Or maybe he'd ridden along with me and had the last of his dreams in the teachers' parking lot, then woken up, climbed out, and walked back to town. But on this day, on the day of my near-labiaotomy, I'd driven him right out of walking range.

You'd think I'd have taken him back to town right away, but no! Not right away. There were greater forces at work that day, namely my fear of what Craig Cribb might do. You see, Craig had flat-out forbidden me to have contact with Hellcat.

Not so many months before, I'd given Hellcat a ride home from the grocery store. It was windy and raining, and he'd stopped me at the buggy depository to ask if I'd drop him off at his cousin's house on my way back into town. I didn't know what to say, so I squeaked out, "Well, I reckon." That was back before I had my full adult voice (because sometimes it takes longer for women to grow up, given that we often go from being a child in our father's house to being a child in our husband's). Anyway, I knew full well that Craig would kill me for picking up a hitchhiker, but I told myself Hellcat wasn't your typical hitchhiker because I knew him. *Everybody* knew him. I waved at him every day—when I saw him kicking through the parking lot of the plumbing supply or leaned up against the wall outside the hardware store, I always waved. (I wave to everybody, but only after my spiritual awakening am I truly happy to see them.) I told myself it'd be wrong to expect Hellcat to walk all the way back carrying his twelve-pack through that storm, and even today I try to give people what they ask for, so long as it doesn't pose a danger to me or anybody else. Hellcat buckled up, and off we went. But somebody saw me. And somebody told Craig.

So surely you can understand the predicament I was in when I found Hellcat in the back of my truck, and me all the way up the road. I couldn't turn around and head home. I had to think things through. And since Hellcat was already snoring in the back, well, I just kept on driving.

MEATY TIDBITS

If you're ever in a position where you need a place to sleep, don't forget that folks often leave their camper-tops unlocked, and it's reasonably common for people to also keep sleeping bags in their trucks, if not to sleep in, then to protect pieces of furniture they're hauling from scratches. If you can find a truck driven by a woman, you'll be more likely to rest comfortably. Back then I kept many useful items in my truck—not only a sleeping bag, but also a box of clothes I intended to drop off at the Hospice Thrift, bottled water, bungee cords, and a flashlight. If you choose a man's truck, and if you get thirsty in the night, you're more likely to have to sip on bourbon, and you might also have to sleep on rancid fishing nets.

If you're married or otherwise committed to a person who exhibits tendencies of a tyrant, like Craig Cribb, try to understand that the person operates out of fear and is mortally afraid of being vulnerable. Think of all the nature shows on TV, how the cornered animal bares its teeth. Tyrants do the same thing. Tyrants are just bratty babies who've grown up, and if you picture a tyrant in a diaper, you won't feel so helpless or nervous in his presence, no matter how loud he hollers. Of course if your tyrant becomes violent, abandon all other advice and hightail it out of there. But if your tyrant's just a blowhard like Craig Cribb, and if he says, "Don't you never talk to Hellcat again. If I find out you've even waved to the son of a bitch, I'll take your keys," or if your tyrant says, "I can still smell him. You stink like shit," don't let it hurt your feelings. Chances are excellent that you don't stink, and moreover, you can't trust a thing your tyrant says until he's cooled down. So do something to comfort yourself. Take a long walk or go see a movie. Before you leave the house, place a baby's pacifier on the tyrant's pillow as a reminder that you see him for the child he is.

3

When I think back to that first afternoon with Hellcat, I realize that he wasn't the only one in a blacked-out stupor. Though I drove my gas tank empty, filled it up, and ran it down again, where I went and what I did beyond that are almost entirely absent from my memory.

How could I pay attention to highway signs when I was so busy mulling over the Craig situation, trying to use our fight after the grocery store incident to figure out how he'd react to my current crisis?

On that day, he'd been hollering before he came in the house: "Damn it, Myrtle. Are you retarded?" (He knew how much I hated that word. That's why he used it on me.)

He slammed the door hard behind him. I was watering a hanging basket of ivy above the kitchen window and didn't turn around. "Did you really let that nigger in your truck?" he asked. (He knew how much I hated *that* word, too.) He stomped into the room so hard it vibrated the linoleum. I stood on tippy toes to reach the ivy, and I could feel how mad he was in the way the floor trembled. I was crying by then, and I'd given the plant too much water. Dirty water trickled down onto the cucumbers sitting on the counter.

"He could've raped you," Craig said. He'd gotten a haircut, too short, and he had a ring of white all the way around his head where the sun hadn't yet burned him. I hoped that the next day, it would scorch him good. I realized right then that he'd seen somebody at the barbershop. Somebody at the barbershop had *told on me*.

"Do you hear me?" Craig said. "He could've killed you!"

"Why would he wanna do that?" I asked, and oh, that made him so much madder.

"'Cause he's a drunk," Craig shouted. He knocked his fist against the dishwasher and accidentally turned it on. "He's probably on drugs, too. I swear, I ought to slap the shit outta you!"

I got a dishrag and mopped off the counter where the water had spilled, then wiped my own eyes with the same cloth, not even thinking. That's when Craig told me I smelled like Hellcat and ordered me to shower, which I did. I turned my face up to the spray and cried like I was dying.

But even then it seemed to me that Craig was the one who ought to be apologizing. He came home every day reeking of dead crabs and armpit, tromping up my carpets with his nasty rubber boots, tracking in God knows what. His feet smelled like rotting bait, all the time, like bait left out in the sun, but I didn't say a word, just sprinkled baking soda in his shoes and washed his fishy clothes. And what'd I get?

That night in bed, Craig turned away and wouldn't talk to me at all. When I tried to move past it and asked how many bushels of jimmies he'd sold, he ignored me altogether. Then just when I was about to fall asleep, he turned over, stuck his finger in my face and said, "What'd you talk about with that nigger?"

"Nothing," I said.

Craig yanked the bedclothes off the bed and went to sleep on the couch. He didn't forgive me for a long time after that.

By the time Hellcat banged on the glass for the second time, the sun was low and pink. He scared me so bad it's a wonder I didn't wreck again. I unlatched the little window to the cab and cracked it enough that he could talk through it. When he slid open the camper window, the air that blew in smelled like throw-up.

"Don't look much like home," Hellcat said, and I had to agree. There were eighteen-wheelers whooshing around us on either side. I think we were somewhere in Pennsylvania.

"I took a wrong turn," I said.

Hellcat nodded. "Need to use the little boy's room."

I said all right, shut my window, and got off the highway at the very next opportunity, where I found a truck stop. It seemed like a good enough place to figure out what to do next. I figured Hellcat might pass for a trucker, and I might pass for somebody who'd arrived there by accident, somebody who didn't know better (which was pretty much the truth). I gave him a ten-dollar bill and told him to get himself some supper, and he staggered away, his boots untied and the laces dragging through the dusty gravel lot.

It occurred to me that I could leave him there. A man like Hellcat was resourceful. He could hitchhike back home, or else he could pass out in the back of somebody *else's* truck. But I knew if I left him he'd be mad. When he got back home, he'd tell everybody he saw, including Craig Cribb.

It occurred to me that I should call Craig and tell him not to worry. Craig's only a tail hole sometimes. Other times he's as sweet as they come. When my parents moved to Florida, he loaded every bit of their furniture and drove the U-Haul without the first complaint, and in all our years of marriage, he's never expected me to take out the trash. I just throw the garbage bags in the back of his truck, and he hauls them to the dump on his way to the harbor. So I needed to let him know that I was safe but waylaid for some reason. I tried to think of a reason, and again, my mind went blank. So I didn't call. I didn't call my girlfriend Dottie, either. I knew Craig would go to her first, and Dottie can't keep a secret worth a diddly-doo. I'd be lucky if she didn't spill the beans about the surgery. My parents were on a cruise ship, a situation I considered fortunate because I didn't want to worry them, too. I pictured Craig looking for me in the house, driving out to the school to see if it was time for PTA meetings, and then asking people at the softball game if they'd seen me. I pictured him finding his momma at The Crab Cribb where she'd still be selling jumbo, lump, claw, or back fin. "You seen Myrtle?" he'd ask, and she'd suck her teeth and say, "Not lately."

I didn't call The Crab Cribb and tell them where I was. Instead, I went into that truck stop and bought a map and some deodorant, a travel toothbrush, and toothpaste. I freshened up in the women's room, cleaning mascara smudges from beneath my weary eyes and using my fingers to try and fluff out my hair. A lady trucker sharing the sink loaned me a couple of bobby pins to get my overgrown bangs out of my face. She told me about a bus station the next town over and showed me on my map how to get there.

I took my supper to go, but ended up throwing it out. I couldn't eat. Hellcat eventually stumbled back to the truck, and I didn't need to look inside his brown paper sack to know he had a bottle in there. I knew the laws against having open containers inside a vehicle, but I blacked that law right out of my mind and told Hellcat to load up. I was getting him a bus ticket home.

Though I wish I could tell you more about the particulars of that day, I'm also grateful for that blessed blackness that kept me numb. It wouldn't last long enough.

MEATY TIDBITS

*If you find yourself in trouble—trouble of any kind—
I recommend wearing down some tire treads. Just riding
around in your car can help you feel less trapped. When*

you pass by different landscapes, see different kinds of homes, businesses, bodies of water, and fields, even when you look at the different kinds of cars on the road, you subconsciously remember how many ways there are to be. The life you're living is one possibility. You have ten thousand other choices.

You don't have to tolerate people who call others hateful names like "nigger." (Substitute "faggot," "wetback," or any other nasty-hearted term.) When words like these enter the air, they change the quality of the atmosphere. If you love someone who uses this kind of language, warn that person. Say something like, "It hurts me when you talk that way. It makes my lungs burn, like I'm breathing poison, and if you don't stop, I'm outta here, buster!" If the person you love understands and tries to improve, you can even give a second chance on a slip-up. But if that person doesn't change, it's perfectly fine to have your lawyer draw up the divorce papers. You don't have to tolerate it, and if you have children, you shouldn't subject them to it. Hateful words will stunt their growth far worse than pesticides or chemicals. It's always okay to leave someone who uses hateful language. You don't need a better reason.

4

Map or no map, the bus station wasn't so easy to find. I couldn't even locate a town, or much of one. I passed a few run-down houses and businesses, an old skating rink, a ramshackle travel lodge, and then some woods. A truck with big tires came up behind me with his lights on bright, stalking my bumper and making me so shaky I'd have taken another pill right then if I'd been able to loosen my grip on the steering wheel. I told myself, "Myrtle, you have every right to be on this road. You have just as much right as that sapsucker behind you." Finally I came to a caution light, and I turned to get away from the truck. That's when I found the convenience store.

It was only desperation that made me stop to ask for directions, because the place didn't look safe. The customers scowled, and a couple of them smoked cigars inside the building. I was the only woman, and it seemed like a bad sign that both the clerk and the cash register were behind iron grillwork. The clerk handed back cigarettes, lottery tickets, and change to customers through a window no bigger than you find in a bank. I knew I shouldn't be in a store like that.

I pulled myself up tall as I could and acted like I owned that store. There's no other way to behave in such situations. I coached myself the whole time, repeating advice I'd been given by an old junior high teacher who'd accused me of slouching:

"Follow your hip bones, not your shoulders," she'd said. I followed my hip bones all the way to the counter before I realized I didn't have a pen or paper to write down directions, so I said to myself, "Myrtle, you'll remember whatever you need to." And I did.

But in spite of my positive self-talk, I couldn't get beyond my panic. I was lost in the boondocks, the *faraway* boondocks. When we finally found the bus station, I understood how we'd missed it driving past again and again. It was no larger than a utility shed. It sat at the edge of an empty gravel parking lot, just off to the side of an old warehouse I'd overlooked before. Really, it was more of a bus *hut* than anything else, and from the faded out schedule posted on the window, it wasn't even clear if the bus still came through. For all my pretending to be okay, studying that bus schedule with my dim-bulbed flashlight just about did me in.

"Don't cry now," Hellcat said. "That ain't gone help a bit."

But I couldn't help it. I walked to the front of the truck and shined my little light on the dent in the bumper. It was the size of a softball, or maybe a big fist, and there were deep scratches that I knew would someday rust. I knelt right down in front of that banged up metal, put my head on the dent, and boo-hooed.

Hellcat followed me. He touched me on the shoulder, but pulled back his hand when I flinched. "See here, it'll be better tomorrow," he said.

"But what about tonight?" I wailed. Since I was already on my knees, I started praying: "Dear Lord Jesus, I am in a tangle," I said (to myself, of course. Even in such desperate straits, I wouldn't pray a private prayer aloud.) "Lord, you gotta help me out."

Hellcat piped up, "Getcha a motel," like it was nothing. Like it's what anybody would do, even Jesus of Nazareth, if he found himself in a similar bind. "You can figure it out tomorrow," Hellcat assured.

"But what about you?" I asked him. Secretly, I hoped he'd

volunteer to start walking home. I thought maybe I could take him back to that convenience store and leave him with the gangsters.

Hellcat shrugged. "I'll sleep the same place I slept last night," he said, and he nodded toward the truck.

Now you might think that moment of camaraderie marked the beginning of our friendship, and maybe it did, if we measure from the earliest, single-celled promise of what later grew. But though I appreciated Hellcat's kindness and though I kept the window open between the truck cab and the camper top and invited him to stick his head through and keep me company, I didn't yet trust him.

I had the shakes by then, and the hiccups, too. Tears kept trickling out of my eyes, and it surprised me, because I'd thought I'd stopped crying. I'd *meant* to stop crying, but the tears came anyway. "I'm so embarrassed," I confessed. I was driving slow and kept hitting the brakes whenever the road curved and I wasn't sure at first which way it went.

"Turn on your high beams," Hellcat instructed, so I did. "Don't feel too bad about having a breakdown," he told me. "Happens to everybody once they figure out how screwed they are."

"I'm not screwed," I whispered.

"Everybody's screwed," he replied. "Up shit creek in a chicken-wire boat. But you'll survive just the same."

MEATY TIDBITS:

When you don't know where you're going, just pretend that you want to be where you already are. You pretend to enjoy other things—Thanksgiving dinner at your in-laws, your nephew's piano recital—and sometimes pretending to enjoy a situation actually brings the joy to it. If you're in an especially difficult circumstance, take notes. Act like you're going to write a daily devotional about it later and need to remember every last detail. This will help you focus, and attentive awareness is the first step to accepting the situation you're in.

We tend to picture guardian angels as heaven-sent caretakers in robes and halos who come to our aid when we're in harm's way. They intercept lightning strikes or spare us from being crushed by the tornado that flattens the rest of the block (too bad the neighbors aren't as well-connected). Sometimes we imagine our beloved dead as our guardian angels—our long-gone granny who makes sure it doesn't rain on our wedding day. We attribute gentle, gauzy love to guardian angels. But sometimes guardian angels are drunk, smelly, and homeless. Sometimes they have dried vomit crusted in their beards. This is something Jesus understood, and it explains his whole idea about turning the other cheek. If your guardian angel slaps the tar out of you, don't hit back.

5

The anxiety I experienced on my journey with Hellcat didn't begin for me there. Even as a child, I was the nervous sort. When hurricanes would bobble along the coastline and weather forecasters would urge us to evacuate, I'd ask my mother if we were leaving. She'd just shake her head and say, "We'll live, or else we'll die in a pile." It seemed just that common and acceptable to her—that if we didn't live (as we someday won't), we'd fall dead one atop the other. No great drama about it.

There's still no great drama in this life, though from time to time, things like having an unexpected drunk man in the back of your pickup truck can make you forget.

We pulled into the motel parking lot, and I took my pocketbook and went into the smoky office, where I had to ring the bell three or four times before an elderly woman with a toothless Chihuahua under her arm rented me a room for thirty-four dollars a night. There were only a handful of other cars in the lot. One of them was on cinder blocks. I pulled the truck right up to the door at the far end of the motel, but when I got out of the truck, Hellcat got out, too.

"I need to use your bathroom," he said.

Naturally, I hesitated. There were people down the way, some Hispanic workers squatting around a grill on the concrete walkway outside their room. I worried about what they'd think if they saw Hellcat go in.

"You've abducted me," he said flatly. "Took me across state lines. I reckon you owe me a hot shower before you leave me out here to sleep in the cold."

I hadn't thought of it as abduction before. Back then, I was only able to see my side of the story, and I considered the situation entirely his fault. (He was the one who had broken into *my* truck, after all.) Still, a shower didn't seem like such a bad idea. I let him in with my big gold key.

The room was old and grimy and smelled like buttered popcorn and mold. There were two double beds, a television set, and a rack to sit your suitcase on. Just seeing it made me wish for a suitcase. The last time I'd been in a motel, my friend Dottie had shared it with me. She'd packed three suitcases for a two-day literacy conference, and we'd skipped the keynote to go shopping. She bought so many clothes that day we had to hide some of them at my house so her husband wouldn't notice all at once.

I said to Hellcat, "I'll leave the door cracked so the room can air out. You go ahead."

While I waited for him, I opened the back of the truck, shook out the sleeping bag, and left him a flashlight beside it. If he needed to pee in the night, he could use it to find his way behind the dumpster. I discovered the box of clothes I'd intended to donate to charity—not quite the same as a suitcase, but the clothes were clean and folded, so I retrieved a shirt for myself and some jeans. I pulled out some clothes for Hellcat, too, some things that were too snug for Craig.

But was it a sin to offer another man my husband's clothes? And should I take them inside, knowing there was a possibility he might walk out of the bathroom wearing nothing but a towel? I wasn't sure.

Instead, I cleaned out the cab of the truck and then sat inside it with the light on, studying the map and trying to ignore my cell phone. I'd turned off the ringer hours before, but in the quiet, I could still hear the vibrations. I didn't answer because I didn't know what to say. I had no explanation whatsoever. Though I understand now that I was buying time to figure out my next move, on that May night, I was mystified about how I'd gotten into the position I was in—and how I was going to get out of it. And where was Hellcat? It'd been half an hour since I'd left him to his shower. I peeked into the motel room and found him passed out on the bed closest to the bathroom, on top of the covers, not even undressed. He hadn't even washed.

I tried to wake him, of course. I nudged him and threw Craig's clean clothes at him. "Hellcat!" I called, "Get up!" But he just said "Uhh," and rolled over.

I ranted and raved, but it didn't matter a bit. He kept right on snoring. Since I knew Craig wouldn't take me back if he thought I'd slept in the same room as Hellcat, I made myself a bed in the truck. I borrowed extra blankets and pillows from the motel room, climbed back there, and closed myself in. But I was too mad to sleep, and I blamed Hellcat for all my sorrows. The madder I got, the more I ground my teeth. I had to consciously make myself unclench my jaw.

The corrugated metal beneath me was too hard, and too cold, and in a while, I started worrying about lice and began itching. I had another crying fit, calmed myself back down, and within the hour, I returned to the office to rent a second room. The place was dark and locked up tight. Even though I rang the doorbell, nobody came.

Back in the truck, I gave myself a pep talk. I wouldn't freeze. It was springtime already. Hellcat slept outside most all the time, taking shelter where he could, so I ought to be able to survive for one solitary night. I tossed and turned, feeling guilty for not calling Craig, and finally I decided to listen to my messages. That was a big mistake, and I ended up crying until my sinuses clogged. My mind went through all the possible excuses. How I wished Craig's daddy were still alive. He'd always stood by me, but he'd died a few years before, eaten up with cancer. I started crying again, thinking of my father-in-law so completely dead and unavailable, thinking of my marriage so totally over, and all because I'd run off to get my coochie cropped so Craig would stop teasing me all the time.

I was doing it for Craig, anyway. The truth was that I didn't enjoy sex very much, but I thought maybe my oversized lip got in the way, made it more uncomfortable and left me irritated. If only I was symmetrical then I could be a better wife! Of course, I was feeling sorry for myself, and at the time I considered myself almost entirely blameless. And, too, it was scary out there in the truck. Lights kept passing by, and I couldn't tell whether they'd spot me. In a motel room down the way, a man and woman were quarreling, and other noises rattled me—truck wheels screeching, peeling off.

Over and over, I considered driving home, but I didn't *want* to go home. I was too *tired* to drive home, too loopy and mad. How in the world had I gotten so *mad*?

Eventually, I ended up in that other bed, in the same room as Hellcat. I lengthened the strap on my pocketbook and put my head and one arm through so it stretched across me and couldn't be easily yanked away. Then I felt guilty for assuming Hellcat would be the kind of man who'd steal my pocketbook. It felt wrong to judge him for being destitute. But surely I shouldn't trust him as much as I'd trust someone with a work ethic and a mortgage, or someone without an addiction!

I told myself his race didn't matter. It always upsets me when people assume that black men are more dangerous than anybody else. But there I was, letting racism contribute to my anxiety.

I had nearly three thousand dollars in cash in my possession—money I'd saved up for my surgery; I didn't want that charge listed on the credit card statement. I'd hidden several hundred in the glove box in the truck, several hundred in my bra, several more in my pocket along with the truck key and the room key, and the rest in my wallet. I kept my clothes on, all of them, and pulled the covers up over my head.

But I couldn't sleep. I kept picturing Craig in our king-sized bed, staring at the ceiling and wondering what had happened. Crying? Sure, he might have cried. He wasn't a bad man. When his daddy was dying and had a hard time getting out on the water, Craig bolted a recliner to the bottom of his skiff so his daddy could still fish and be comfortable. Poor Craig. I knew he'd never remember to bring in the mail. He'd forget to feed Purvis, the cat, but Purvis would eventually remind him, batting at his nose in the night until he did it.

In the next bed, Hellcat's snores vibrated in his throat, rattling like a coffee grinder. I wasn't even sure Craig knew how to work the coffee pot. Ordinarily I fixed the coffee the night before and set the timer.

"Hellcat," I called. "Roll over." But he didn't. That made me miss Craig, too, because Craig always rolls over when I tell him he's snoring. He apologizes, too, says "Sorry," and flops onto his belly, and even though he doesn't remember it the next day, it's one of his sweetest features, that he's sorry about waking me up with his snores.

"Roll over!" I hollered again. No use. I tried to find a comfortable position but the mattress was lumpy, and every time I shifted, the bed squeaked. It seemed like it was sending me messages in the screeches. I'd adjust the pillow and the bed would say, "Go home." Or I'd lift my legs to get the covers tucked tight around my ankles, and the bed would moan, "Craig Cribb."

At one point, I got up to look behind the drapes and make sure there wasn't a camera crew filming me for a reality TV program. I thought maybe Craig had planted Hellcat to see what I'd do when confronted with an unexpected situation. Maybe the whole town was in on the joke, even the convenience store clerk who'd given me directions to the bus station, even the motel owner's Chihuahua. I pictured them all watching me on a camera somewhere and laughing. But there was no camera, and I scolded myself for acting like I was Numero Uno, like the world was rotating around me.

The red lights on the clock clicked minutes away, then hours, and it seemed like I'd never sleep again. My head was stuffed from crying, my jaw ached from tension, and I had the beginnings of a headache pounding behind one eye. "Please sleep," I whispered to myself. "Please sleep." And I did, eventually, when my busy mind couldn't figure out any other way to make it to morning.

MEATY TIDBITS

It's human nature to try to avoid suffering, but it's not always possible, and it's not always easy to determine if the thing you think will prevent suffering actually will. Take, for instance, the decision to answer your cell phone. You don't have to answer it every time it rings. A phone is a convenience, not an obligation, and you can elect not to answer it. Even if it's your husband, wife, or otherwise beloved, you can weigh the suffering you'll undergo if you answer it against the suffering they'll undergo if you don't. Think, too, about the wrong-headed things you might say if you answer at the wrong time. You have the option to turn off your phone or leave it in your vehicle while you sleep. You don't have to listen to it ring all night.

Whenever it looks like there are only two ways to handle a situation—answer the phone or ignore the phone— force yourself to think of a third way. In my case, I waited until The Crab Cribb was closed and left a message on the answering machine there, saying that I was safe but had been called away by a family emergency. I knew that Craig would get this news before daylight. His mother would open up early for the watermen, put on the coffee, and put out the biscuits. She'd check messages while Craig loaded crab pots onto his boat. He'd find out that I was safe just before morning, about the same time I finally fell asleep.

6

I've had two migraine headaches in my life. The first was completely painless. I was in third grade, and our class had taken a math test and exchanged papers to grade them. As the teacher called out the correct answers, I discovered I could only see the left-hand side of the page. It turned out that I'd taken only half of the test. Half the world was clear to me, the other half lost in a vibrant glowing. My mother picked me up from school and took me straight to the doctor, where, to her relief, they ruled out a brain tumor and diagnosed me instead with a migraine.

The second time, I was in the motel room with Hellcat, where it would have been preferable to see just half the picture. (The half that he wasn't in.) But this migraine hurt. Before I woke up, I was dreaming of a jackhammer, pounding, pulverizing, vibrating in my teeth, and then a deep voice throbbed against my skull bones: "Hey there," it said. "Hey!"

At first I thought it was Craig telling me I'd overslept. Then I opened my eyes. The instant I recognized Hellcat, I sat upright. It wasn't a bad dream, after all! That's when the nausea hit me, so down I went. *Don't throw up,* I said to myself. *Don't throw up.* I could feel my pulse beating in my head, relentless, and the light from where he'd opened the drapes came in through my closed eyelids. It was like looking straight up at the sun.

"Close the blinds," I said.

"You sick?"

"My head," I said.

"I gotcha some coffee," he said. "You want some coffee?"

"Uh-uh."

"Let me get you some water then," he offered, and as he walked to the bathroom, his footsteps kicked me in the temples. He turned on the water, and it deafened me, Niagara Falls in my ears. Still, I was glad for the water and managed to sit up a little when he returned with it. I had the last of Craig's pain pills in my pocketbook, so I went ahead and took it.

"Might be from grinding your teeth in the night," Hellcat suggested. "That'll give you the headache."

I passed back the cup and said, "I don't grind my teeth."

"Oh, yes, you do," replied Hellcat. "I let you sleep an hour after I got up, and you've gnashed 'em like sinners in Hell."

I lay back down and tried to take deep breaths. I didn't like it that he'd been watching me sleep. Something about it seemed sinister. I looked at Hellcat again, but I couldn't really see him. He was a red shadow of himself, glowing. If my head hadn't hurt so much, I would have sworn I was dead and gone to the devil. Maybe I *was* in Hell.

Somehow I made it to the bathroom before I threw up, and before I came back to bed, I got a wet hand towel to put over my face. I knew I needed to take some medicine—at least some ibuprofen—but my stomach was so queasy and so completely empty by then.

"Reckon it'll hurt your head if I turn on the television?" he asked.

"Please don't," I said.

So he sat there doing nothing, and I tried to figure out what had caused the migraine. Stress? Too much crying? Tooth-grinding?

Or could it be a reaction to Craig's pills? Trying to figure it out made my head hurt worse. It could be any combination of those things—or even a smiting from our Lord and Savior Jesus Christ.

Hellcat offered to get me some breakfast, but of course I said no. He was hungry, and I wanted him to leave, anyway, so I gave him a twenty and tried to sleep. I couldn't tell if the hurting was in my eyes or in my skull bones, in my ears or in my teeth. I couldn't think about anything then, except one breath after the next. Even though I was awake, I was also dreaming. Crazy memories twiddled around dreams. My mouth tasted like metal, and I remembered going to the dentist when I was little and getting silver caps on my teeth to keep them from rotting out. I'd taken medicine as a baby that made my teeth soft, but my momma claimed that with those caps I had a mouth full of jewels. I smiled too big to everybody, thinking my teeth were silver dollars, but a boy outside the dime-store said I had a mouth full of nickels. I was waiting there to take my turn at riding the pony, the money in my hand, and the boy who was riding back and forth told me to go away or he'd pull out my teeth and use them to ride the pony forever.

Then I was on the pony, and I rocked there until I became a pony. There was a coin slot in my shoulder and Craig put his money in. He'd ride me forever, until my silver spring wore out.

Then I was caught in the spiral of a great silver spring. The silver spring began to rust as I circled it, round and round, and my mouth tasted like rust, and the circling made me sick again. I barely made it to the trash can before I threw up.

When Hellcat returned, he brought me soda crackers. He'd been watching television with the woman who ran the motel, and even though she was sorry for my illness, she'd sent him back with a warning that we either had to check out or pay for another day.

Thirty-four dollars seemed like a small price to be able to stay in that bed, and that's where I remained. I kept down some ibuprofen, but it didn't help. I hoped if I was very still, the medicine might coat my head, and I visualized medicine in my blood, and I pictured it silver and washing across my brain with every heartbeat.

My mouth tasted tingly, like there were silver bugs inside it, and then I could feel them, stainless steel and crawling down my throat. The bugs became the heads of pins, the round ones used in Biology where Craig and I were lab partners, dissecting a frog and labeling its parts. Except now he was dissecting me, and I was opened up from the inside, pinned to the table by my skin, my labia exaggerated, supersized, stretched over my thigh and pinned down on the other side. The light was so bright above me, and Craig didn't know I could see it. He thought I was dead, but I wasn't. I was right there watching him take me apart, organ by organ, weighing and judging every part of me.

That evening, when I couldn't stand it anymore, Hellcat put me in the truck and drove me to the emergency room. I was throwing up into a trash bag by then, and they put me on a stretcher. I gave Hellcat my pocketbook, wallet and all, and he dug out my insurance card and handled all the paperwork. If he'd walked off with my wallet and all my money, if he'd taken the truck and driven to Kalamazoo, I wouldn't have cared a lick. That headache stripped everything but the pain.

The doctor asked some questions, checked my eyes, had me touch my nose, and told me to roll over. He gave me a shot in my backside, a long and burning, wonderful shot that shut down my head altogether. I didn't even correct him when he said, "Come on in here, Mr. Cribb, and keep her company. She'll be feeling a lot better soon." I sat there thinking, "Do I really look like the kind of woman who could be married to a homeless, freckled black man named Hellcat?" I sat there thinking, "Did Hellcat really stand right there and watch the doctor give me a shot in the behind?" But any horror at these notions left almost as fast as it crossed my mind. I didn't even argue when Hellcat took the chair beside my bed and waited with me until the pain subsided.

Then I was so relaxed that I couldn't even sit up in the truck. All my muscles surrendered. I rode in the back on that sleeping bag. Every now and then I'd hope that Hellcat had a driver's license, or I'd hope he wasn't driving drunk. But I was so sleepy by then and so happy to be free of pain that I didn't even care that he was smoking in the cab of my truck. I didn't care when he stopped to pick up a case of Colt 45s on the way back to the motor lodge. I was too out of it to complain.

MEATY TIDBITS

Most of us think that the ideal state is to be free of pain, but in fact, pain's a part of life. When you find yourself in pain, you might as well collapse into it. Think of how a jellyfish eats. A jellyfish is all mouth, and in one gobble, the whole shrimp is inside that big old floppy head. Let pain take you the way a jellyfish takes food. Picture pain as a jellyfish that folds right over you and lifts you inside, makes you a part of the pain itself. You can squirm all you want, but it won't do any good. Holler till your throat's sore and you end up with a sore throat. It'll be better if you quit fighting. Just remember, you don't have to be scared. The jellyfish eats and excretes from the same huge mouth, and in time, you'll get spit back out, transformed.

If you feel like you deserve to be punished, you will be. If your husband, wife, or otherwise beloved isn't around to fume and fuss over your mistakes, your body will take up the cause and make certain you suffer. Now before you send me threatening emails or claim, "Myrtle, you can't possibly mean that my deep vein thrombosis is my fault," just let me say, of course not. Not every illness has a psychological root. But some illnesses do. So I urge you to consider in what way in your own life you punish yourself when you're not getting the punishment you've come to think you deserve.

7

Back in the motel room, I dozed off and on while Hellcat watched *Animal Planet*. I was groggy and loopy from the shot, though no longer in pain, and no longer nauseated. Hellcat woke me up when the pizza came. He'd ordered a big one, and he sat it down on my bed and went to get drinks.

At some point he'd cleaned up. He'd shaved and put on the fresh clothes I'd thrown at him the day before. He wore Craig's jeans low on his hips, but they were still a little too short. In the absence of a belt, he'd cinched them up with a piece of braided cord—a perfect match to the motel-room drapes. He'd traded in his boots for a pair of leather flip-flops Craig's sister had sent for his last birthday (like Craig would ever wear flip-flops). Those had also been in the box for the Hospice Thrift. Hellcat's feet looked flaky and gray.

When he offered me a Colt 45, I saw that he'd filled our little sink with ice and was using it to chill the cans. He'd already drained several. It seemed the alcohol was making him talk in slow motion—or else I was under the effects of medication more than I thought.

"Just water," I said, and he fumbled with the plastic cups, filled one for me, and brought it to my bedside. His hand looked huge when he offered me that cup. His fingernails were long— almost as long as a woman's—and I wondered if he liked them that way or if he didn't have any clippers. I must've been feeling better by then because I shivered with the thought, *I don't even know this man.*

Since we didn't have napkins, he grabbed us each a hand towel from the bathroom, and then he plopped right down on the foot of my bed and opened that cardboard box, and we ate. This pizza was cut differently from pizzas at home, not in triangular wedges but on a grid, in squares and rectangles, smaller at the edges and bigger toward the middle, and I remember thinking it'd be impossible to know how much you'd eaten given this strange pizza design. How could you control your portions when they weren't equal?

Hellcat's beard-nibblets had made him look dirty; without a beard, he looked a lot younger. I kept staring at him and trying to remember how long I'd known him. I didn't remember him from childhood or even my teenage years. I thought back on all the bums I'd known. There was old Joe Barnes, who banged on doors and asked for money, but he'd had a heart attack down by the pier and died. Homicide Hank had killed his stepfather many years before, when he was still a child, then was released at age eighteen and came back to town on a scooter. But he'd disappeared, too. Maybe he was back in prison. Had I ever seen Hellcat with Joe or with Hank?

I pretended to watch *Animal Detectives,* but really I was doing an activity I sometimes assign my students, having them cluster all their thoughts and memories around an image to generate ideas for stories or posters or comic strips. My image, of course, was Hellcat.

Hellcat had helped Craig's daddy rake pine straw to put around the azaleas. He'd helped him shake the pecan tree most years until his death. My father-in-law considered Hellcat harmless and always sought him out when he needed bricks stacked or gutters cleaned. I'd seen Hellcat fishing off the pier plenty of times, walking along the railroad tracks. I'd seen him hanging out by the propane tanks outside the grocery store.

Finally, I settled on my first memory of Hellcat, which had taken place at the town harbor on one of the most shameful days of my life. About six or seven years into our marriage, Craig had bought a new boat and motored it from across the bay where he'd purchased it into his slip at the harbor. His old boat had belonged to his uncle, who'd worked the water until he'd had a stroke, and after the uncle had died, Craig had used that boat another ten years, crabbing and tonging for oysters, fishing for red drum and black. It looked like it'd been in a knife fight, battered by storms and years of crab pots heaved and tossed, scraped by rocks and barnacles and God knows what, and I was glad when he decided to replace it. His old boat had been called *The Lady Renee*, named for the girl he'd dated through eleventh grade, until she'd moved off to Texas. So I didn't even mind that we had to take out a second mortgage to get this new boat. I was ready for a name change as much as anything else.

I was out at the harbor and waiting at the docks with a bottle of champagne to christen Craig's new boat the first time I saw Hellcat. He was leaning against the pilings with a water-hose, hoping some waterman would pay him to help clean up. I remember he made me nervous—not because he was black but because he was out of his element, not even realizing that the hose he'd borrowed belonged to one of the biggest bigots in town. He could get into a heap of trouble acting like he had a right to use it.

But when that shiny new rig came in, I forgot all about the stranger standing there. I couldn't swallow past the grief that knotted up in my throat. I couldn't even wave back at Craig, who was grinning and acting the fool. Because the name on the side of the new vessel read *The Lady Renee II*.

"How could you?" I asked Craig, right in front of his crew. They were still tying up, and my words were too loud and broken when they left my throat.

"What?" he said. "How could I what?"

I pointed at the name, painted in big calligraphy letters. "How could you do that to me?"

He laughed a little. All the boys around laughed. "Honey, I didn't do nothing to you," he said. "Everybody knows me by my boat's name. You can't just go changing the name of your boat."

"Why not?" I asked him.

It was an awkward moment and one that still makes me blush—because it happened in front of everybody: his crew and the harbor master and the mayor, who was about to take his family out fishing on the pontoon. In front of Hellcat, too, though Hellcat was the least of my worries on that day.

Maybe I shouldn't blame Craig for what he said next because I'd put him on the spot. But he chuckled and said, "I reckon you want me to call my boat *The Lady Myrtle,* do you?"

I wish I could tell you that I came back with some witty retort or even that I chunked that champagne bottle at his depth finder, but I didn't. The bottle slipped right out of my fingers and made a soft little plunk into the bay, bobbing beneath a jellyfish.

Hellcat had been there to witness my humiliation that day. Now he was scarfing down the pizza crusts I'd left behind.

"Did you know Homicide Hank?" I asked him. "Or was he gone before you got to town?"

"Who?" He brushed off his hands, took the pizza box over to the trash, where it didn't fit, and settled back down on his bed.

"Never mind," I said. We went on watching TV for a while, and I wondered if he remembered that day when he'd seen *me* for the first time. He'd probably been too drunk to recall it.

When he got up to retrieve another Colt 45, I asked him, "Do you have a criminal history?"

"I beg your pardon?" he said.

"Do you?"

"Not hardly," he said. "Do you?"

"No," I said, and I stared at him until he admitted to a

couple of DUIs and disorderly conduct charges. I wondered if there was anything else he wasn't so forthcoming about.

He shrugged. "Last time I went to jail they charged me with Negligence."

"What's that?" I asked him, and he explained that it was a word the police used to keep the homeless off the streets. I tried to figure out what a homeless person might be negligent about. Hygiene? Or throwing away his trash? Could littering be considered Negligence in legal language? "No violent crimes?" I asked.

He cut his eyes my way and shook his head. "I'm gonna try not to take offense. After I've done my best to look after you, get you medicine, food. Shit," he said.

I felt bad then. It's not right how people treat the disenfranchised, me included. It's not right to assume that because somebody has an alcohol problem, he's necessarily a blemish on society. "Hellcat," I said. "I'm sorry."

He ignored me. He kept watching a woman from Minnesota investigating some chained up, starving dogs, trying to find their owner, who was nowhere in sight. Could he have a dog somewhere that he'd neglected to feed?

"Hellcat," I said. "Really. I'm sorry."

He snapped at me then: "Why do you keep calling me that, anyhow?"

"What?"

"Hellcat," he said. "How come you keep calling me that?"

"It's your name, isn't it?"

"No," he said. "My name's Vetiver Faulk. Not that you ever bothered to ask."

For a minute, I was scared. What if I was on the run with some homeless man I didn't even know? Had I been so drugged up I'd mistook him for Hellcat? He was watching TV again, and so I peeked his way and determined that he was, indeed, Hellcat, unless he was Hellcat's identical twin.

"Vetiver?" I said. "Well, did they call you Hellcat in the Navy or something?"

"Weren't in the Navy," he said.

"Oh," I said. "I thought you must've flown one of those airplanes. Isn't there an airplane called a Hellcat or something?"

"There's a bomber from World War II," he said. "You think I look like a pilot?" He crumpled his can and threw it at the trash. It bounced off the pizza box and landed on the floor. "You think I look that *old*?"

"I figured you were in Vietnam," I said.

"Wouldn't have me," he said.

"In Vietnam? I thought they took anybody. Were you too drunk?"

"No, Myrtle," he said. "Believe it or not, I haven't always been a drunk."

"Sorry," I said.

"One of my nuts didn't drop," he told me. "Back then, a fellow needed two nuts to go to war. I wasn't man enough for 'em."

Then I wasn't sure what it meant that he'd used the word "nut" outright, like it was nothing. It might have been different if he'd said "testicle." Craig always said "balls." "Don't crush my balls," he'd say. I wondered what it meant that Hellcat had said "nuts."

"I should call you that, then. Vetiver. I never heard that name before."

He softened. "It's a kind of grass," he said. "Grows in Haiti where my grandma was from."

"You're from Haiti?" I asked.

"My grandma was from Haiti," he said. "Ain't never been there myself."

"I figured your people were from Africa," I said.

He snorted. "Reckon some of 'em's from Africa. Some of 'em's from Haiti. Most of 'em's from South Carolina."

"Named after the grass," I said. "That beats all."

"Ain't so special," he said. "You named after a tree."

"I'm named after my mother," I told him, and I tried to imagine my mother out there on her cruise ship, dancing on a deck somewhere. What would she think if she could see me in a motor lodge with a black man named Vetiver Faulk?

"Then your mother's named after a tree," Vetiver said. "You can call me Hellcat if you want to," he said. "You won't be the first."

MEATY TIDBITS:

Sometimes it's good to try on a new name—not necessarily for keeps but just as a way of seeing how the old name fits. Once a year, try going off somewhere that people don't know you and introducing yourself by a different name. If your name is "Lisa," see how it feels to be "Roberta." You might also take a trip with a friend and agree to call each other by a different name or by no name at all. Names are perceptions, which are assumptions. It's clarifying to be rid of them.

Even if you think you're not a prejudiced person, you probably are. While you might tell yourself you don't care whether a person's skin is brown or beige or yellow, deep inside you have an entire file cabinet of impressions about race. You inherit impressions from your parents and their parents before them, from the people you spend time with, whether you like them or not. The more you consider their beliefs wrongheaded, the more you run the risk of swinging too far the other way (as if you can make up for another person's judgments). I was so busy trying not to think Vetiver was dangerous because he was black that I might have wound up sharing a motel room with any black man, just to prove a point, and that wouldn't have been too smart of me, now would it?

8

At the time of my accidental pilgrimage, I taught special needs children at the elementary school, a job I'd been doing for more than twenty years, and I considered it an exhausting and thankless vocation. I loved the children (most of them, anyhow), but resented all the policies and protocols that made it next to impossible to focus on the students' learning. And I was ready to pinch the heads right off of the parents.

In short, I was burned out.

I'd arranged in advance to have a substitute teacher for the day of my surgery and the day after. It wasn't until the third day that I needed to take additional sick leave. I rose early and called the school before the secretary arrived, so I could leave a message on the answering machine. My lesson plans were on the computer, and my classroom assistant knew what to do, anyway.

I made a lot of noise in the motel room that morning, turning on the news and running the blow-dryer, figuring surely I'd wake up Hellcat—Vetiver—and we'd get an early start to the Amtrak station where I intended to buy him a ticket. But he'd gone through most of the case of malt liquor and was sleeping it off. He didn't even wake up when I found the little black loop of hair on my underarm deodorant. I squealed outright and wiped it off with a Kleenex. At that point, I'd never shared deodorant with another person, not even with my best girlfriend, Dottie, and she wouldn't have left behind hairs, anyway.

My plan was to call Dottie around 7:20. She'd be in the school parking lot then, having a cigarette in her Camry. She had bus duty that week, which begins at 7:30, and she'd have to sign in beforehand, probably about 7:28, and it would take her a few minutes to get her bags together and walk in. I figured five minutes was plenty of time to reassure her, but not enough time for her to ask unwanted questions. Dottie was the only one in the world (except the medical staff at the doctor's office) who knew about my intentions to "go symmetrical."

So I roused Hellcat—Vetiver—and told him to get up and get ready, and I went out to the truck to make my call.

Dottie answered right away. "Where are you?" she asked me. "Girl, are you all right?"

"I'm okay," I said. "I'm fine." But my voice was mostly a whisper.

"You don't sound fine," she said. "What happened? Did something go wrong?"

"Not really, " I said. "I'm just real tender," and even though I was lying, I choked up a little, and I realized I *was* tender—though not between my legs. I didn't exactly mean to make it sound like I'd had the surgery. I was trying to be vague until I figured out how to tell her the truth.

Dottie said, "I'll come to you. Damn! I should've gone with you in the first place."

"No. Really—"

"Why didn't you call?" she asked. "I've been worried sick!"

"I had such a bad headache," I said, and even though that part was true, it sounded like such a puny excuse that I kept talking. "A side effect of the anesthesia, I guess." (I told myself at the time that it wasn't an outright lie if I counted Craig's pills as a kind of anesthetic.) "There was an aura around everything, Dottie, and I couldn't even see the numbers on my phone." The words kept rolling on out.

"Oh, honey," she said. "I'm so sorry." I could hear her shuffling around, collecting her papers. "Well, how does it look? Did he do a good job?"

"I don't know," I told her—and then I almost confessed to everything—that my decision against the surgery was *nothing* compared to finding Hellcat in my truck and managing to *stay with him* for the next 48 hours. But Dottie had bus duty, and there wasn't time to get into all that. So I said, "I haven't really seen it yet."

"Why not? Are you bandaged up?"

Again, I didn't *exactly* lie. I didn't say anything at all. But I knew full well how Dottie would interpret my silence.

"Doesn't that make it hard to tinkle?" she asked.

"Not really," I said. And what I said next, I just can't explain: "Not with the catheter."

"Catheter!" she said. "Oh Myrtle, I feel awful. Let me get a sub! I'll get a sub and come right to you."

"Don't," I said. "I'm all right. Don't be upset."

"Where are you? I need the address so I can put it in my GPS. Let me get a pen." She dropped the phone, said, "Damn. Myrtle? Are you still there?"

"Shhh," I said.

"I can't stand to think of you all by yourself!"

"I'm not by myself," I said. "Not entirely."

"What?" Dottie asked. "What do you mean?" and her whole tone changed. "You're kidding," she said.

I'm not proud of myself for leading Dottie down this pathway of deceit, and yet it achieved my primary aim, which was to distract her from insisting on coming to my rescue. I knew that Dottie'd been having an affair with the girl's softball coach at the high school. She'd met him back when her daughter played for the team, and they'd been doing the dirty for a good five years. (And before you judge her, just remember that you haven't walked a mile in her Mootsies Tooties and hush). So I knew that Dottie'd be comforted and delighted to think of me sharing her sinning ways.

She laughed a little then and said, "Myrtle? Seriously? You're *with* someone?" The car door slammed as she headed towards the office. "Not that I blame you, of course."

"Yes," I said. "And he's taken very good care of me." I didn't miss the irony in telling the truth smack in the midst of my amazing growing lie.

"Well, I swear," she said. "It's not that doctor, is it? Are you sure he's not a perv? Seems to me like any man who makes his living cutting up va-jay-jays must be disturbed."

"It's too complicated," I told her. "I'll have to call you later. But don't worry about me because I'm fine."

We'd been friends a long time already, and Dottie knew what was coming next. "Don't you hang up on me!" she said. "Myrtle!"

"If you see Craig, *don't say a word,*" I said—and pressed the red button quick. Out there in the truck, I closed my eyes and took some deep breaths. Dottie. My best friend in the world, and I'd fed her a line of bull and hung up on her, too. I toot-tooted the horn for Vetiver, and while I waited there, I dialed Craig's number—I knew he'd be on the water and wouldn't have a signal—and I left him a message explaining that my Great Aunt Doris had taken a turn for the worse, and with my parents on that cruise ship (a lucky break, since Craig couldn't reach them), I was the only one to sit vigil. It wasn't even a good lie, since I don't have a Great Aunt Doris, but by that point, what the hell.

MEATY TIDBITS

About all this lying—well, it isn't ideal, obviously. No enlightened being in her right mind would encourage you to lie, and I'm no different. I certainly don't think lying exemplifies a mature spirituality, and if you're reading these devotions, I know that's what you, too, are seeking. I just don't think lying is always as bad as it's made out to be. A lie will have to be dealt with in one way or another, but so will the truth. Some spiritual guides will tell you the truth is always best. I disagree with those kinds of teachers. The truth is sometimes best. Sometimes not.

An almost-lie, a deliberately vague statement that you know your listener will misinterpret, is a lie. But it's also a boring and weak lie, and if you're not telling the truth, anyway, you might as well make up a good story, one somebody would enjoy dwelling on, sharing, and even repeating. If you're going to lie, at least make it good enough that one day when you're in a nursing home with nothing to do, your friends already dead and your hands too shaky and arthritic to crochet, at least you can think back to your lie and know you gave people something juicy to gossip about.

9

The Amtrak station was busier than I expected. Though I'd hoped to park in front long enough to run inside and pay for Vetiver's ticket, it didn't work out that way. We had to leave the truck in a dark garage across the street and take concrete stairs to the ground floor, then wait for the light at a busy intersection and still rush to avoid cars as we crossed. All this activity upset my natural balance, and as I marched into the big open room and up to the ticket line I was thinking, *What am I doing here?* I'd never spent much time in cities and didn't know how to negotiate them. I kept checking my watch, adding up miles, calculating hours, and thinking I could be back home by dark if I got out of there soon. Yet all the time, another part of me knew that if I intended to drive home that same day, there'd be no reason to get Vetiver a ticket.

I kept obsessing, too, about how to get out of the city by myself. My sense of direction has always been rickety, and Vetiver was the one who'd helped me find the train station in the first place.

He hadn't talked much on the early part of the drive that morning, though he'd given gruff instructions: "Stay to the right" or "Three miles 'til the turn." Then out of nowhere, when we were almost to the depot, he asked me why I'd left Craig Cribb.

I told him that I *hadn't* left. I certainly hadn't left him on purpose, and Vetiver asked, "Did Craig Cribb hit you?"

"Of course not," I said. "Craig's never laid a hand on me."

"Good," he said. "I just thought maybe that was why you left. That'd make sense, if you left because he smacked you around."

"Well, he didn't," I said, and I honked my horn at a pesky little sports car trying to cut me off. In a way, I was glad to have somebody to honk at.

A little bit later, for no apparent reason, Vetiver started talking about water and how it moves, how sometimes a tree falls across a creek and dams it up, and smaller branches and leaves and straw and trash accumulate and strengthen the barrier. "But after a while," Vetiver said, "the pressure builds. The dam bursts. The water flows again. You catch my drift?"

"I reckon," I said.

"Sometimes your fear might keep you in an unhappy place for a while," Vetiver continued. "But after a time, when you get miserable enough, when that pressure builds up, you blow, Girl. You just blow." He looked at me seriously and said, "You blew, didn't you?"

For some reason, that made me blush.

There in the ticket line, I couldn't stop worrying about what would happen when Vetiver was back in our little town. Would he tattle on me? I was scared to let him go back without being there to defend my reputation.

Vetiver asked, "Where you heading next, now that you'll be rid of me?" and I panicked again, not because I didn't know where to go, but because I realized that I didn't want to be by myself.

I felt very small then, and the train station seemed cavernous. Everything rang loudly in my ears, and I wished I could be a little mouse and scurry away somewhere. But where? Where did all the other little mice scurry?

The only thing familiar was Vetiver. So that's how I decided to wait with him for his train, which wasn't scheduled to arrive for a couple of hours.

"You don't have to wait," he said, but I told him I didn't

mind, that I appreciated how he'd taken care of me the day before, with my headache and everything.

"You'd have done the same for me," he said, and then I really felt terrible, because I wouldn't have. A hundred times I'd driven by when he looked sick without stopping to see if he was all right. Oh, I waved, of course, to be polite, but kept right on about my business. Once I even found him passed out in the drugstore parking lot. Like so many other people, I just rolled my eyes, went directly inside, flopped down at the lunch counter, and ordered my hamburger, assuming that he was drunk and that the man who drove the Pepsi truck would drag him into the shade where he'd sleep it off. For all I knew, he could've had a medical condition, a seizure disorder, and I'd chalked it up to disorderly conduct and secretly wished the police would haul him in.

Remembering this, I felt so bad I bought him a puzzle book to do on the long ride back. He was going to have to switch trains in Washington, D.C. I gave him more money so he could visit the snack car. I even gave him money for beer. And then I begged him not to tell anybody he'd seen me.

"I won't say nothing under one condition. Long as you tell me why you're running off."

"I'm not running off," I said again.

"You got an awful lot of money in cash for somebody not running away."

I squirmed in my plastic Amtrak chair. "You can't tell anybody," I said.

"I won't," he promised.

"I need some surgery," I confessed. "I was on the way to get it when I found you in the back of my truck."

He looked at me like he didn't know whether to believe me or not. "Nothing too serious, I hope."

I shook my head.

"You pregnant?" he asked.

"No!" I said. (Craig and I tried for a while to have children, but he had slow swimmers and blamed it on me. It was a tough season in our lives, but nowadays, I'm glad I didn't have children with Craig. He can't even scoop the cat box without gagging.)

"Seems like your husband ought to go with you when you need to get some surgery," Vetiver said, and that made me sad for a lot of reasons. I hadn't given Craig the chance to go with me. Even if I had, he probably wouldn't have gone, but you never know. More than likely, if I'd been home when I had that migraine headache, he'd have called his momma to drive me to the ER.

I couldn't stop thinking of myself as a creek with a big old oak tree named Craig crashed down across it, heavy and asleep, too heavy to roll off, clogging me up.

Then, too, I was sad to have almost cut off my pouty lip in the first place, poor old droopy thing that it was. Vetiver must have seen the complication cross my face because he said, "Are you lying to me?"

"Do I look like a liar?" I shot back, and he cackled outright. It was the first time I'd seen his teeth, and they were long and tinted blue.

"Long as you're feeling so generous with your money," he said, "let's buy a little time on the Internet. I haven't checked my e-mail in three days."

There were two computers off to the side of the wall, and you could rent them in fifteen-minute increments by paying the snack bar attendant and getting a password. I hadn't known Vetiver knew how to use the Internet, and frankly, I was surprised. I didn't know many homeless alcoholics, but as a group, I didn't expect them to be computer literate, not that I'm proud of my stereotypical thinking. I'd seen Vetiver going in and out of the library, but I figured that's where he went to stay out of the weather or use the bathroom. So you can imagine my surprise when he logged on and read the e-Courier sent out by our town manager, the same e-Courier I found in my own mailbox. This time it wasn't the usual stuff about bagging up your grass clippings, conserving water, or being on the lookout for rabid wildlife. This particular issue, dated several hours before, mentioned my disappearance. It had quotes from Craig saying, "Myrtle would never up and leave like that. She's too good a woman and too good a wife. And besides that, she don't even have a Great Aunt Doris." According to the notice, Craig had contacted the authorities, but the police had declined to pursue the case because there was no sign of foul play. Anyone with information was asked to call The Crab Cribb or the Town Office.

"Poo, poo, poo," I whispered, and I might have kept on saying it like a holy chant except that right then, another e-mail came in. An update. According to this e-Courier, they had tracked my insurance card. I'd used it twice the day before, in a hospital and a pharmacy, and according to descriptions from the attending physician I'd been accompanied by an African-American male with freckles and a big red afro. The e-Courier alleged that the description resembled Mr. Vetiver Faulk, also known around town as Hellcat, who had failed to show up for his appointment with his social worker two days prior, and asked that anyone who had knowledge of either of our whereabouts come forward immediately. There was an additional notice printed in bold italics, saying that Mr. Faulk had a nonviolent criminal history, but that he may be holding me against my will.

"Shit, shit, shit," Vetiver said, and he might have kept on saying it like a holy chant except that I noticed a train pulling in, heading north instead of south, and it was a close call, given that we had to trade in his ticket and get a new one for me, but we made it.

MEATY TIDBITS

It's natural to panic when you realize that you don't know what you want. When you're looking at a train table and you see all those destinations, it can throw your mind into overdrive; it can trip up all your circuits. When you're not sure what you want, you can easily get lost in the not-knowing. If this happens to you, simply STOP. Take a deep breath, and eliminate the things that you know you don't want. You don't want Wyoming or Louisiana. You don't want Home. Just these bits of information can keep you off the wrong train. Knowing what you don't want can be guide enough. It can keep you from making the wrong choice, even if you're not yet sure what the right choice is.

Whenever you feel little and furry, like a mouse in a great big room, find a wall, crouch against it, and watch people walk by. Chances are excellent that they won't see you. If you feel silly doing this, pretend to be looking through your pocketbook or backpack and glance up occasionally to notice that nobody's paying you any mind. They're all trying to catch their own trains. After a while, your legs will get tired from the squatting, and it'll feel better to stand up and behave like the adult that you are. It's important to remember that when you are still and off to the side, whether crouched or standing tall, you're practically invisible. There's no need to crawl behind a kiosk or make a spectacle of yourself, and in fact, if you do this, you'll become conspicuous. Think again of mice. You rarely notice a mouse sitting quietly against a wall. You see the mouse when it scurries across the floor. Just seeing it scurry can make you want to stomp it, or find a broom and pummel it. So when you feel like scurrying, stop. The secret to staying safe is to quiet yourself down.

ACTIVITIES FOR
FURTHER GROWTH

» Take a trip to the largest parking lot in your town, and examine the bumper stickers you find on the vehicles. See if you can identify the traits of the driver by the kinds of stickers on the cars. For example, if you see a sticker that says "Teach Peace" or "Girlz Rock," you might deduce that the vehicle belongs to a woman; whereas if you see emblems of little boys peeing on Chevys or Fords, you might assume the vehicle belongs to a man. (If you had to break into one of these cars to sleep for the night, what would be the potential payoffs and obstacles of each?) Select a sticker that seems to reveal something about the owner's age, gender, race, or demeanor, and then wait until the shopper returns. Were you right or wrong? Don't beat yourself up if you guess wrong. It's a wonderful surprise to see how often we are wrong.

» Make a list of the tyrants you've known in your life and then see if you can identify what would be gained by maintaining a close relationship with that person. Does the tyrant provide the opportunity to live in a nice neighborhood? Does the tyrant come with Caribbean vacations? In my case, Craig Cribb took care of all the decisions in our marriage. I didn't even have to decide which brand of mayonnaise to buy. Apparently a part of me liked having someone tell me what was right and wrong, where I could go and where I couldn't. It made life simple. Often the people who remain in relationships with tyrants are mistaken for stupid—but that may not be true. It may be that they simply haven't yet taken responsibility for their own lives. If you discover that you're currently living with a tyrant, don't feel too bad about it. You're not powerless; you're choosing it, whether you can identify the reasons yet or not.

» Recall all the vacations you've been on and consider whether and how they enhanced or hindered your personal growth. Don't forget that though we tend to think of vacations as physical trips, a vacation is actually a mental state. For many of us, the idea of going to a new or faraway location allows us to see things differently, but it can be equally rewarding to take a vacation in your own home. To do this, you simply have to break your routine. If you ordinarily drink orange juice for breakfast, try lapping it up from a saucer like a cat. The taste buds at the tip of your tongue are different from those at the back, so your orange juice won't taste the same. Drag your mattress out onto the porch and sleep there. The quality of your dreams will change. Put up your Christmas tree in June for just one night; then take it down again. You will like yourself better when you've spent some time away.

» Examine your relationship with Guilt. Are you an addict? If you find yourself wracked with remorse, often sick, and feeling pitiful, you're probably still putting yourself at the center of the universe and giving great importance to decisions you've made. As they say in the big city, "Get over your bad self." The punishment you suffer isn't necessarily deserved. Just because you *feel* guilty doesn't mean that you *are* guilty. Ask yourself, too, if you've been punished enough. If the answer is yes, treat yourself to some ice cream, a round of mini-golf, or an Italian lover if you can find one.

PART TWO

10

Before I go on with my story, let me acknowledge once again that I'm not your average visionary. Craig reminds me regularly that I can come across as a fruitcake and a nag. (He used to joke to friends that he was married to a little nagger woman.) It's true that I may not be the most eloquent in my speech, but then neither was Moses. It's a simple fact that I have practical and spiritual advice to offer, learned through my own mistakes, and if I didn't think it could help somebody, I'd get a pedicure or learn the Fox-Trot instead. Dottie read a draft of this manuscript and pointed out that my advice ranges from the serious to the sentimental to the downright wacky. "What's so wrong with that?" I asked her. I know that some folks would like it better if this devotional was coming from *either* a psychologist *or* a theologian, *either* an intellectual *or* a mystic—but that either/or thinking can box you in as surely as a bad marriage (or too strong an affiliation with a political party). I'm not the either/or type. Rather, I'm a down-home kind of know-it-all. But all my knowing comes through firsthand suffering, and I wouldn't be doing my duty if I didn't pass along what I've learned.

Up until that day when Vetiver and I hopped the northbound Amtrak, the only train I'd ridden had been the one at Tweetsie Railroad, where we vacationed when I was a girl. The Amtrak was dirtier and more crowded. We couldn't find seats together but managed to stay in the same car. Vetiver took an aisle seat next to a businessman reading his paper and left me to climb across a woman blowing bubbles in her sleep a few rows up. I settled there as the train pulled out, slow at first and jerky, then faster and rocking.

I had a therapist once—back when I couldn't get pregnant and needed help dealing with the grief—but she died, so I couldn't have called her even if I'd had my cell phone with me. I'd left my phone in the truck, attached to the little charger plugged into the lighter. I'd thought I'd be right back and hadn't even brought along my sunshades. My only possession was my pocketbook, so I plundered through it and stuck it under my seat. No magazines, no cards to shuffle and spread out on my food tray, but at least I had my wallet, with credit cards and cash, though the credit cards were in Craig's name, too.

If you can believe it, I felt calm—for a little while, anyway. Hopping on that train had been the first clear decision I'd made in a very long time. I wasn't coerced into it, and I wasn't ambivalent. Though I hadn't intended to leave behind the truck, I'd parked in the garage where I could pay by the hour or by the day, so it didn't really matter that I was taking this unexpected trip.

In a while, Vetiver came over and asked if I wanted to join him in the dining car, and so I went. Ordinarily when I travel to see my parents down in Florida or to see Craig's sister and her family over in West Virginia, I carry so much stuff that it's hard to lug it all around. And why not? If you're in a truck, you might as well have an extra bag for shoes, a coffee pot so you can have a cup in your room each morning and pretend to be sleeping late while you muster your courage to face blood relatives. But on the train, I was glad to be traveling light. I could sling everything I had over one shoulder, and so I did and left that seat for good.

We had burgers and beers, a number of them, and though I don't ordinarily drink beer, on that day I found it just right.

Sometimes you need a little vacation from the person everybody thinks you are. I decided I might as well take one.

"Call me Roberta," I said. "Just for today."

"What the hell for?" Vetiver asked. He was still in a bad mood over the insinuation in the e-Courier that he'd kidnapped me.

"Just for shits and giggles," I said. Up until that point, I wasn't very adept at cussing, either, but I figured I might as well give it a try.

"This all seems like a game to you, does it, Roberta?" he asked. "You tell me what you think's gonna happen to me when you decide to go back home to Craig Cribb."

"Nothing," I said. "What do you mean?"

"They'll string me up from a tree," he said. "For taking off with a white woman."

"No, they won't," I said. "Not in this day and age."

"Where we come from?" he said. "Shit. I'm a dead man." He reached into his pocket for a cigarette, then, realizing he couldn't smoke on the train, he said, "Save my seat," and made his way to the little bathroom at the end of the snack car, where he almost certainly lit up anyway.

When he returned, I made him a promise: "I'll tell them you didn't abduct me," I said.

"They'll get me in the night, take me off in a boat, tie cinder blocks to my ankles, and throw me over. Don't you ever watch *America's Most Wanted*?"

"Don't talk like that," I said. "That kind of thing doesn't happen in the world we live in today."

"You think we live in the same world?" he said. "Me and you?" He crushed his beer can in his hand. "You're a good woman," he said, "But you've got your head up your ass. You disappear and they start looking for you right away. You can't even run away if you *try*." He laughed and shook his head. "Me—if I disappear, won't nobody come looking for me unless they think they can put me in jail."

He had a point, but what gave him the right to get mad at

me about how the e-Courier interpreted our absence? It wasn't my fault. And why did men always get to be the ones doing the abducting? Why wouldn't it cross anybody's mind that *I* could do the abducting? It made me want to go out and kidnap somebody just to prove that I could.

Then I remembered that I already had, sort of. "Vetiver," I said. "I won't let them blame you for this."

He looked at me and shook his head, and even though I knew he didn't believe me, he said, "Thank you, Ro."

We stopped for a long time somewhere underground— maybe New York City—but it didn't look like much. We could have been anywhere with a lot of rails and people and shadows and exhaust fumes. Vetiver got off for a cigarette, and I went with him. When we returned to the snack car, a family had taken our table, and we had to share a booth with an Amish-looking couple having lemonade. The train started rolling again, and we passed concrete walls and graffiti, chain-link fences, the backsides of garbage dumps. We stopped in small town after small town, letting people on and off the train, and Vetiver and I continued our conversations. In hindsight, I probably shouldn't have encouraged his drinking, considering how much he'd had the day before. But while it wouldn't have been possible for Myrtle T. Cribb to guzzle alcohol on the Amtrak, it was easy enough for Roberta. The more I drank, the easier our conversations became.

That day, I discovered things about Vetiver I hadn't known. He'd been married long ago to a woman who'd died suddenly of an aneurysm. He had a grown daughter in Charleston, South Carolina, who worked as a phlebotomist at the VA hospital, but they didn't keep in touch. He seemed sad about it and said it was because she'd paid for his rehab and had even gotten him a job helping her husband with his construction business. But he'd backslidden, fallen off the wagon. The Amish-looking couple shook their heads sadly at this news. Vetiver pulled out his wallet and showed us all her picture, encased in a cloudy plastic sheath. In the picture, she was only eight or nine.

I found out that he'd worked as a maintenance man at our hospital for a while. My tongue was loose from all the beer, and so I asked if he'd gotten fired, but he said he'd quit. "I could hold down a regular job if I wanted to," he said. "I just don't want to anymore."

"You see, that's the problem," I said. "That's why people in town think you're a bum. You have the ability to work, but you don't. You lack ambition." Maybe I was slurring by then. It's entirely possible. But I didn't want the Amish-looking couple to confuse me with someone like Vetiver.

"I got plenty of ambition," he replied and swallowed down a burp. "Just not ambition to punch a time card every morning." He shrugged. "You think my life counts less than yours because you work forty hours a week?"

"No," I said, and then I changed it to, "Maybe. It seems to me like able-bodied people should work and not live off the taxpayers." It came right out of my mouth. I'd heard Craig say it a thousand times.

"I work," he said. "I don't ask for nothing for free. 'Course if I had a regular job, I'd be lost it by now." He motioned around the train car, as if I'd forgotten that we weren't having this conversation at our local pub.

"If you had a regular job," I told him, "Then you'd have a regular house with a regular bed, and you wouldn't have been sleeping in my truck in the first place, which by the way, you were doing for *free*." The Amish-looking woman turned her face to the window and pretended not to hear, but how could she help it? The man looked down and used his pocketknife to dig at the stains beneath his nails.

Was it the content of our conversation that made them uncomfortable, or the fact that I was holding my own in an argument with a man? I could've never talked that way with Craig. Craig expected me to go along with whatever he said—

even to believe it. I wasn't allowed to disagree with Craig, but here I was having a disagreement with Vetiver. In a way, I enjoyed it.

Vetiver said, "You think you do things the right way because you do them like everybody else. See, to me, looks like you can't think for yourself. In other countries, they don't work forty hours a week."

"In Japan they work fifty," I said.

"And then commit suicide," Vetiver added. "I ain't talking about Japan. I'm talking about the Mediterranean where they know that everybody needs to sit under a tree at lunchtime and play a game of checkers. Or in Mexico where they get 'em a nap in the hottest part of the day." He looked at the man seated next to him as if he was hoping to get an "Amen," but the man didn't acknowledge him at all.

"Those are stereotypes," I said. "You're just trying to justify your laziness."

"Lazy?" he said. "Lazy? You a fine one to judge me. Who are you or any of these people to judge me?" He made a big swoop with his arm, and even the people at the other tables looked away. "I know something you don't," he claimed. He was talking loud by then. "I live in the groove. Most people go about their lives worrying and fighting. I quit fighting and worrying a long time back, and I get what I need."

I picked up his beer can—don't ask me why because Lord knows I was emptying my own that day—and I said, "Is this what you need?"

"I might drink too much," he said. "I might drink till I throw up. Then along comes a possum to eat it. In the wintertime, if it wasn't for me, that possum might starve to death."

I must have made a terrible face because Vetiver laughed and added, "When's the last time you fed the possums, hmm?"

"Never," I said. The Amish-looking couple stood, wished us a good trip, and hurried away to their assigned seats. When we ordered another round, a couple at a nearby table across the way gave us a dirty look and got up, gathering their things. "Go on back to your seats, " Vetiver said. "See if anybody around here misses you." He winked at me, and I said, "Yeah. Take a hike." It sounded ridiculous, I know, but it had been a very unusual day, and by then everything seemed funny.

When the train attendant cut us off, Vetiver and I walked all the way to the back of the train where there wasn't a caboose at all. There were shelves back there where the checked baggage had been stowed. We climbed up onto those shelves amid suitcases, him on the right side and me on the left, and took a little nap.

MEATY TIDBITS

Once you're an adult, you don't have to stay in your assigned seat on trains or airplanes. If you don't like your seat, get up and move. When you're in a restaurant and the hostess seats you next to another table, even when most of the room remains empty, it's perfectly fine to request a different table, one near a window, for example. You're a paying customer. You have the right to make your wishes known. If you go to a motel and they give you a room on the first floor, you can ask to be moved to the third. You can ask for a room with a balcony or a room that faces the woods rather than the highway. You have nothing to gain by being accommodating all the time, and the worst thing that will happen is that you'll be denied your request. Big deal. If you're lucky enough to know what you want, then you should do your damndest to get it.

If you don't consume alcohol very often and decide to get rip-roaring drunk, then it's probably a good idea to wait until after dark to order your first round. That way when you've had enough, you can just go to bed. At least by that time most hardworking people are at home and not watching you stumble through their evening commute. When you get the spins, you don't want it to happen when you're plopped down at a little table in the food court of the train station, trying to soak it up with chicken fried rice. If you decide to get drunk at all, expect that whatever emotions you're trying to gulp down, they'll come surging back up along with all that beer.

11

People swarmed—people of all kinds, speaking languages I'd never heard, pulling suitcases, hauling guitar cases, rolling elderly parents around in wheelchairs. There were people gated off in little waiting areas and people dropped right onto the floor reading paperbacks. Over loudspeakers, mechanical voices announced which trains were now boarding. We leaned against a wall beside a gift shop and tried to orient ourselves. "Where to now?" Vetiver asked.

"I don't know," I replied. "But we need to find a bank so I can get a cash advance. Otherwise they'll be able to track us down with the credit cards. Craig's name's on all the accounts."

"You're kidding me," Vetiver muttered. "You white women could learn a thing or two from black."

"What do you mean?" I asked. I fished out my credit cards, wondering how much the interest would be. I made a mental note to keep track of how much I owed Craig.

"A black woman does her banking in her *own* name," he said.

I wasn't sure what he meant by that, but I knew it wasn't a compliment. "That's racist," I said.

"Call it what you will," Vetiver replied.

So we found an ATM and took some cash advances, and then I sat on a bench and bent the cards back and forth, back and forth, until they broke in the middle, while Vetiver went to check the train schedule and see if there was anything headed west in the next hour or two. I started thinking about those charms girls used to wear, lock and key charms, or two halves of a heart charms. The girl wore one half and gave the other half to her boyfriend to carry on his key ring (though it probably wound up in the glove box of his truck). I kept half of each credit card and threw the other in the trash bin. Part of me thought I should mail Craig his halves, but I didn't have an envelope.

When Vetiver returned, I was caressing my half of the credit cards and sobbing onto my knees.

"What's the matter now?" he asked.

But how could I tell him I missed Craig? If I'd been home right then, we'd have been crashed out on the couch watching Bill Dance fish for bass on the big-screen TV. Craig's stinky feet would be propped up in my lap, and he'd be saying something like, "Baby, go get me some ice cream."

"I've ruined everything," I said. "I'm such a dumbass."

"That ain't no way to talk," Vetiver said.

"It's true. I mess up everything." And in that moment, that's how it seemed. My life had been completely manageable before. Unfulfilling—yes—but also manageable. Now I was in some big city up north with a homeless Haitian-American freckled black man with one nut.

"See here," Vetiver said. "That's how life is. One day everything's fine. Next day everything's gone to hell. That's normal."

"I've ruined my life," I whispered. "And Craig's life, too."

Vetiver cocked his head and said, "You know, you're feeling awfully powerful for a drunk woman."

It turned out that we'd walked to the wrong part of the station. The ticket counter where I'd sent Vetiver was for the commuter rail and wouldn't get us farther than the suburbs. As we backtracked, we discussed the possibility of getting a sleeping compartment with bunk beds and riding across America, visiting national parks all along the way. But when we stopped at a kiosk to check the fare, we discovered it would cost a thousand dollars, literally, and we didn't want to blow that much cash, especially now that the credit cards were gone.

By then my head was hurting again, and I worried about my migraine coming back. I couldn't make a decision about whether to get on a train at all.

"Maybe we should look for the YMCA," I said. "Don't they help you out at the YMCA?"

If Vetiver was frustrated with me, he didn't let on. "Let's take us a walk," he said, and so we went out into the night air, and we found a little café where you could use the computer while you drank your coffee. Though we had to wait a while, it was worth it because I sobered up considerably. I had a muffin and wrote a postcard to my parents. Then when the computer freed up, I sent an e-mail to Miss Hattie (Craig's momma—he didn't have an account of his own), to Dottie, to my principal at school, and to the Town Manager all at one time. In the e-mail, I made it clear that I'd left of my own accord, and I apologized for the pain I was causing. I resigned from my job and my marriage, effective immediately, and promised to be in touch again when I could. I cried and cried while I wrote it, and Vetiver stood there and rubbed my back and patted me through my hiccups.

"What else should I say?" I asked him.

"I don't know," he said. "Maybe something about the moon and stars."

"What about them?"

"I don't know," he said. "Maybe something about how from a distance, the stars look close to the moon even when they're far apart. Maybe something about how even though you have to go away for a while, you'll be as close as a star."

So that's what I wrote.

On the way back to the train station, we decided to buy coach seats and ride out to Yosemite. Neither of us had ever been, and it felt good to have a destination in mind. But we approached the station from the wrong side, from the bus terminal, and when we stopped to get our bearings, we ended up smack-dab in the middle of a group of old hippies who were suddenly moving toward a bus.

"Let's go," the driver called. "We're running late."

On either side of us, people hurried to board—we were right in the middle of them, practically corralled—and when we tried to step out of the way, a thin old woman with long dark hair pulled into a knot shooed us forward.

"We're not really with this group," I said.

"Of course you are," the old woman replied. She had murky turtle eyes.

By then we were almost at the bus door. I took Vetiver's arm to pull him aside, but he whispered, "Think like a hobo, Myrtle. Free ride." Some fellows in turbans hurried around us to climb up, bumping us with carry-ons and apologizing.

"Come along," the old woman insisted.

"Really," I said. "We don't belong here."

She laughed hard at that and nudged me up the steps. "Haven't you ever heard the phrase 'Go with the flow,' kitten?"

Of course I'd heard it, but it sounded different in her accent. She was from somewhere else—maybe Portugal by way of Tennessee. I couldn't figure out if she was Appalachian or some kind of gypsy swami. Maybe there were gypsy swamis in Appalachia, anyway, but did they call grown women "kitten"? The bracelets on her arms tinkled behind me.

I thought, "Wait," but I kept moving. The bus was almost full. I said, "We don't have tickets," and at that the old woman said, "But you still have seats." She pointed to two at the very back. Before Vetiver and I got to them, the bus rolled away.

MEATY TIDBITS:

Our imaginations are limited by what we've been exposed to in the past. It's hard to imagine anything that you haven't dreamed or sensed or seen. In the movies, creatures from the future look like dinosaurs; aliens are nothing more than men with bulby-heads— plus chlorophyll, minus genitals. Add bat wings, spider legs, or the fins of fish to regular old homo sapiens, and voilà! You've created a superhero. We imagine new things by combining bits of the world we already know. But mystery requires us to abandon even our own imaginations. When you're suddenly on a bus with strangers and they all believe you belong there, no amount of imagination can explain it. At first you think you're dreaming or hallucinating. Then you think you have Alzheimer's. Ultimately you give yourself over to the mystery. There are things you simply can't explain. Not everything has to be accounted for.

If we didn't have astronomers to tell us differently, we'd believe that with a strong wind, the stars could bump right into the moon. Thanks to physics, we know something about distance, something about the vastness of the universe, but not a whole lot. For all practical purposes, two stars can be as close or as far away as your own two eyes.

12

The old woman wore a print dress, tennis shoes, and a fringed shawl over her shoulders. She moved up to the front, said some words to the bus driver, and then began making her way down the aisle, checking on each passenger as we drove out of the lighted city and into darkness. She seemed to know everyone. With some passengers she laughed quietly. With others, she simply patted shoulders and turned out overhead lights. Bit by bit the bus grew quieter.

"Where do you think we're going?" I asked Vetiver.

"No telling," he said. "Don't make much difference." He reclined his seat and leaned his head against the window.

"Maybe it's a cult," I whispered. "What if we're being recruited?"

"Maybe we're going to Nova Scotia with the Rotary Club," he said and yawned.

"What about Yosemite?"

"We'll go there next," he told me, and then he fell asleep.

I sat there in the dark. I'd been sleepy before, but now I was awake. I kept thinking about the Nazis, how they rounded up the Jews, led them into the showers where they gassed them, and I thought maybe we'd be gassed. But the anxiety wouldn't stick. The old woman was nothing like a Nazi, and beneath the anxiety, I was actually excited.

Only a few hours before, I'd lamented leaving Craig and my comfortable life. When I thought of Craig by himself, taking his bath before bedtime, when I thought of him trying to wash his own back without having me there to soap it, I still choked up a little. But I didn't choke for long because another part of me felt like I could go anywhere. By morning, I could be anywhere, and I didn't have to do anything except allow things to take their course.

It took a while before the old woman made it all the way back and eased herself into the seat across the aisle from me. "I'm Sister Esther," she said. "And you're?"

"Myrtle," I whispered.

"Pleased to have you with us, Myrtle," she said. "Get some rest. We won't be stopping again until morning."

"Where are we going?" I asked.

"Down the freeway," she teased. "Over the river and through the woods."

"There's been some kind of mistake, though," I said. "We just happened to be standing there by the bus . . ."

"Nobody *just happens* to be anywhere," she said kindly. "Just because you don't know why you were there doesn't mean it was random." There was a satchel beside her, and as she searched through it, I considered her words.

If getting on the bus wasn't random, then maybe nothing was—my botched attempt at labia surgery, my abduction of Vetiver, my migraine headache that kept me on the lam, or even farther back, my marriage to Craig in the first place. "It wasn't random?"

"No, kitten," she said. She was unlacing her sneakers by then and replacing them with bedroom booties. "And I'll tell you something else. There's no such thing as a mistake."

But she had to be wrong about that. As soon as she said it, all my mistakes leapt up from the pit of my stomach into my throat, a great mass of mistakes, too big and hard to swallow away, and tasting like soured beer. I pictured Craig's momma handing Craig the print-out of my e-mail, and I saw him reading it. I knew for the first time what an Adam's apple must feel like because I had one of my own. In my mind, I watched Craig fold that paper three times and stick it deep into his pocket.

"If you could see the last week of my life," I said to the old woman, "you'd change your mind about mistakes." My throat went starchy, and water gathered at the edges of my eyes.

The old woman reached across the aisle, took my hand, and squeezed. "You're on a journey," she said. "You've found your guide, but now you must trust."

"Are you my guide?" I asked.

"No, dear," she said. "Your friend," and she nosed towards Vetiver, who was snuffing in his sleep.

"I don't think *he* could be my guide," I whispered. "He has an addiction." I realized as I said it that I probably had beer breath. "We're not really together," I said, "I mean *together-together*. I have a husband."

"It's okay," the old woman said. "Few people are married to their guides. Your relationship needn't be physical in order to be intimate."

She clicked on her overhead light, flipped my palm over, and stretched my arm upwards like she wanted to warm my hand there. I had to turn my legs into the aisle to reach.

She brought her face close to my hand, studying it, and she traced a line with her finger, sighed, and said, "the heart line." Then she assured me that I knew how to love and said I'd deepen my loving all my days. But how could she make that claim, when I'd left my husband? I didn't ask her then because she was already speaking of my passion, pointing out the fleshiness of the pad beside my thumb. I didn't tell her Craig and I hadn't made love in six months. There wasn't much passion left between us. I'd started undressing in the bathroom so he wouldn't see my body. But I didn't want to hurt Sister Esther's feelings. She clearly fancied herself a psychic, and I didn't want to make her feel like a bad palm reader.

When it came to my head line, she remarked on its length and downward slant. She said that I was an artist, and I didn't tell her that the only art I did was finger painting with my students, or sometimes a cross-stitch pattern in the evenings before bed.

Then she touched the curved line that started out so thick and chained, but gradually faded into nothing.

"And that line?" I asked her.

"That's your life line," she said.

"What does it tell you?" I asked.

She took my hand again and squeezed. "You died years ago, dear. But today you're starting again."

MEATY TIDBITS

Transition times are freeing. When you're in a transition, don't fret about where you're headed or where you've been. Allow yourself to be suspended between places and obligations. Certainly this is the case if you're on public transportation—bus, plane, or ferry—or if you're stuck in your car waiting for the train to pass. You can also enjoy the freedom of being in-between when you're waiting in line at the grocery store or the drive-through at the bank. Rather than getting frustrated and impatient, treat those times as opportunities to rest. Take a deep breath and be thankful that somebody up above knew you needed a little break.

I've seen it embroidered on pillows that the best times in life are spent with friends, but I'd argue that sometimes it's better to hang out with strangers. You get different information from strangers. Without even intending to, strangers let you know how you're being perceived. When you're seated next to a stranger at a wedding, when you find yourself stuck in an elevator, when you drop off your dry-cleaning and they've hired a new clerk, remember that each person will react to you in a way that can show you something new. And your interactions can also show them something new.

13

At some point in the night, I slouched into Vetiver, and when I woke, my face was nuzzled against his shoulder. But since he was wearing Craig's Rockfish Classic T-shirt, and since he'd showered the day before and didn't smell especially ripe, I rested there for a few minutes before I remembered that he wasn't my husband and I wasn't at home. I straightened quickly, only to find there were people standing in the aisle beside me, waiting for their turn at the toilet. "Good morning!" a very chipper bald man said, his toothbrush stuck out the side of his mouth. He had a long brittle beard that frazzled out about mid-chest, and the sea turtle on his shirt looked like it was peeking out from behind all that hair.

"Morning," I replied and wiped my eyes. Out the window, the branches of trees streaked the gray sky.

"Almost there," he said. "We'll be there for breakfast!"

"Great," I said, without mentioning I didn't know where "there" was.

The bus was barely moving. We were climbing a mountain at such an angle that it seemed we might all have to get out and push. I was glad for the rock wall outside my window because, on the other side, the world dropped away.

Once we began our descent, we had the opposite problem, going too fast as we zigzagged down narrow roads, bouncing around bends, through trees just getting their new leaves, so yellow in their greening. As we climbed a little dirt road, Vetiver jostled awake. We crossed over a wooden bridge and jerked down the other side along the river, where at last we pulled into a shady, makeshift parking lot already occupied by a few vans and cars.

Since Vetiver and I didn't have any luggage, we helped Sister Esther with hers. As we hiked through the woods, she told us about the place, which had once been a 4-H camp but was now a spiritual retreat center. "We'll get you outfitted after breakfast," she said. "There's a Lost and Found where you can find a change of clothes."

On the way to the main building, we passed cabins amid the trees, and Sister Esther explained that those were for workshops and classes. The cabins that still housed participants were farther down the trail. We entered the main building, a lodge with big exposed beams and wooden tables and benches in long lines, and that's where we had our morning meal—thick slabs of brown bread with rhubarb and prune jellies and weak hot tea.

I was still trying to get a straight answer about what kinds of things went on at this camp when a woman with frizzy gray braids asked Vetiver if he'd join her crew. This woman had a hound dog with her, right there in the dining room, and the dog sniffed around for table scraps while she explained that she was looking for someone with a strong back to carry five gallon jugs of water to each of the workshop spaces. So off he went with this woman and her dog.

I wandered around the edges of the room and pretended to be okay. I found the bathroom and took the opportunity to wash up and brush my teeth. But even my hygiene was going downhill by then. My toothbrush was gritty with dirt from the bottom of my pocketbook. There were pinecones and bird bones in a little bowl on the back of the toilet, and it worried me for reasons I can't explain, except to say that at that time,

I was accustomed to potpourri and Lysol in bathrooms, not dead birds.

In the main hall, people greeted one another, laughing, hugging. It reminded me of the first day back to school every August, how we gathered for coffee and donuts before the in-service assembly, commenting on each other's suntans or hairstyles. (Then I always snuck off with Dottie to gossip about who'd gained the most weight.) The people at this place didn't dress like elementary school teachers, I'll tell you that! They wore tie-dyed tent dresses, loose linen pants, T-shirts and shorts. They wore sandals with canvas straps. They seemed to know each other already, or at least each group knew its members. I told myself that feeling like an outsider would help me back in the classroom when a new kid arrived, knowing no one, dreading recess. It helped to think I'd be able to make use of my discomfort, until I remembered I didn't have a classroom to return to.

Finally the bearded, bald man from the bus came up and took my hand and shook it for a long time, "We haven't officially met," he said. "I'm Carl," and he looked so proud to *be* Carl that it calmed me. He smiled, and I smiled, and he asked, "Is this your first time here?"

I nodded.

"You're gonna love it," he said. "Whose workshop are you in first?"

"I'm not sure," I said.

So he led me over to the bulletin board where they had lists of cabin assignments, workshop assignments, and work assignments. I was actually relieved when I didn't find my name on any of these lists. For a while there, I'd started to worry I might be losing my marbles.

Carl dug in his beard, found a crumb or a scab, and flicked it away. "Huh," he said. "There must be some mistake," but Sister Esther overheard and rushed over. The metal rims of her dentures showed as she said, "Uh, uh, uh" and Carl laughed too, and together they recited, "No such thing as a mistake."

Sister Esther said, "They've taken the place of the Locklears."

"Oh," said Carl.

"The Locklears?" I asked.

"They had to cancel," Sister Esther explained to Carl.

"Too bad," said Carl.

"But as you can see, they sent Myrtle and Vetiver in their place."

"We don't even know the Locklears," I said.

Sister Esther wrapped an arm around my shoulder and squeezed. Then she consulted the clipboard she was carrying and muttered to herself, "Campsite N—the Locklears reserved Campsite N." She flipped a page and said, "Vetiver's already been claimed by the maintenance crew. We can use you on the clean-up crew after dinner. And your first workshop will be—" She looked up at me and squinted, then turned back to her clipboard and began scribbling. "Balancing stones by the creek," she said.

"There isn't a stone-balancing workshop scheduled for today," Carl told her.

"There is now," Sister Esther replied. "Could you look in the storage room for bedrolls and sleeping bags and deliver them to Campsite N, Carl?"

At first he looked puzzled. Then he smiled and gave Sister Esther a hug. "Of course," he said. "I'd be happy to."

Then Sister Esther took my arm and said, "Let's find the Lost and Found."

MEATY TIDBITS

Whenever you go to a place where they make decorations out of pinecones and bird bones, there's a pretty good chance they'll also expect you to save the carcasses of dead bugs to display in the windowsills. There's a pretty good chance that when someone finds a leaf with an interesting vein pattern, they'll pass it around the lunch table so that everyone can say, "Ohhh," or, "That reminds me of a trail I hiked on Grandfather Mountain." When your turn comes, take the leaf in your hand and appreciate it. Even if it seems silly, it's nice to look at a leaf. In our daily lives, we probably don't spend enough time looking at leaves.

Trends in clothing are cyclical, and if you find yourself wearing something outrageous, assure yourself that you're on the cutting edge of fashion, and let it go. We get so caught up in wearing the style of the day that we seldom consider whether we actually like rubber shoes in bright colors with airholes over the toes. We wear them because that's what we see in store displays and magazine ads. If there comes a day when you dress yourself from a Lost and Found box, wearing garments left on the limbs of trees after someone has gone skinny-dipping, then you'll have the opportunity to enjoy being mismatched. Once we become adults, we seldom overlay stripes with polka dots the way we did when we were four. In my case, Sister Esther tossed me a couple of T-shirts and a drawstring patchwork skirt, and though I'd never have been able to survive in such a getup on the Eastern Shore of Virginia, it made a perfectly appropriate wardrobe at the Raven Creek Center for Spiritual Enlightenment, which is where it turns out I was. If the clothes you wind up in seem unattractive, soften your gaze.

14

That afternoon, we balanced stones, Sister Esther and I. There was no one else in the workshop, and there were no instructions, only a creek bank and the ordinary things you find there—limbs and logs and reeds and frogs, dirt and rocks and weeds. For the longest time, Sister Esther wandered along the edges of the water, picking up this and that. I assumed I was early and others would be coming, but nobody else came, not Vetiver, not Carl, not the woman with braids or her dog.

In a while, Sister Esther squatted by the water's edge, and so I walked over to see what she'd found. She'd taken a stone and set it against another stone, and she puzzled over them, like she thought they might fuss about it.

I didn't know if I was supposed to help her or not. I thought maybe I should collect some rocks, and so I did. I found a larger rock sticking up from the water, and I pried it free with a stick and carried it, dripping, back to Sister Esther.

I didn't want to interrupt her, so I stood there waiting for her to notice me. But after a while my hands got tired and the mud running down my arms dried cold, so I asked, "Want to use this one? It's bigger and might make a better base."

When she looked up, she seemed surprised. She smiled and said, "I have my stones already. You start with that one."

At least then I knew that we weren't working on the same

rock sculpture. Why was it so hard to get basic information? If Dottie'd been there, she'd have poked fun at me for waiting on instructions. Dottie would've come right out and asked: "What are we supposed to be doing? You gotta tell me the rules if you want me to play your game!"

I always admired Dottie for being able to say what she meant. My whole life, words had tangled up in my mouth so that they never came out the way I intended. Craig used to pick on me about it, saying that's why I worked with "the retards." Of course it hurt my feelings for him to talk that way about my students. I tried to teach him to say "disabled" instead of "retarded," and then I tried to teach him to say "differently abled" instead of "disabled." But I could never make him understand why it mattered. He'd say, "Honey, I'm just doing it to get your goat. How come you take everything so seriously?" But I did take it seriously.

I found another rock and sat it on top of my first one. Sister Esther was still over there playing with her same two stones. Lord, the things that Craig would say about *her*!

So I took off up the hill and down the path, where I selected several more. The long skirt came in handy. When I picked up the hem and made a sling of the skirt, I could carry multiple rocks back to the water's edge. I dumped them out by my little rock snowman and went to work balancing them.

By then Sister Esther had stretched out on her belly and looked to be about to kiss her stones. I took apart my first sculpture and put a wider, flatter rock on the bottom. The next one fit securely above it. The third and fourth were a little wobbly but they held. "How far should I go?" I asked Sister Esther.

Again, she acted surprised to see me. In her world, there were only those stones. "As far as you like," she said.

That's what I did all afternoon. I made little stone heaps, and to tell the truth, it wasn't a bad way to spend a day. I dug some out of the creek bed and kicked some up from the trail. Sometimes I worried about whether I was doing it right. I've always been the sort of person who has trouble with obvious things, figuring out how to get the ice out of a drink machine, for example, or how to turn on a gas pump. Once when I took Purvis to the vet and the waiting room was full, I sat right down on the scale, not realizing that it *was* a scale or that it was flashing my weight for everyone to see. So I knew I might be balancing my rocks all wrong. Still, I stacked and arranged them.

Some of the rocks were smooth; some were jagged. Some were solid colors and others were striated with different shades of gray and clay. I rolled them around in my hands, knocked them against each other, listened to the sounds the different shapes made, and while there was never really *a lesson*, I think I figured out the point: Too often as we grow older, we lose our sense of joy. That day as I balanced stones with Sister Esther, I realized I'd forgotten how to play. I also realized that in spite of all his flaws, Craig had not. Even as a little boy, Craig loved being out by the water, breathing the briny air, chasing crabs into their holes, jumping off the dock and swimming back to shore. He found a way to make his love of the bay his life's work, and in this way, Craig is more spiritually evolved than most of us.

I got lost in rocks. I pounded and tossed, built a stone xylophone and tapped out songs I'd long forgotten. I thought a lot about my students, too, and wondered why I'd never given them time to balance rocks. Back in college, I'd chosen Special Ed because I believed Special Ed students were *special*, and I thought that if I could help those children recognize and utilize their unique gifts, the entire educational system would be better for it. But as the years went along, I'd fallen into the same kind of thinking as most everybody else, seeing Special Ed as rehabilitation, trying to make those students more like the average thinkers. No wonder I'd burned out. I decided if I ever went back to teaching, I'd stop worrying so much about test scores and spend more time with puzzles and games and music and art. If I ever taught the solar system again, I'd take those children to the bay, have them choose rocks and shells to represent the planets and the sun. I was working on a model of the solar system myself when Sister Esther appeared there before me, saying it was time to head back.

As we were leaving, we passed the place she'd been working. There were just the two stones there, a small one on the bottom and a larger one balanced above. It seemed impossible how they balanced, with the top stone's weight not evenly distributed but cocked sideways almost, perched on the crooked tip of the smaller one below. How could the small stone hold up the larger one? It would have looked like magic, except I knew it'd taken her all afternoon.

MEATY TIDBITS

There's no one way to balance stones. The right method depends on the desired outcome. Back in the olden days, stones were used to mark important places or passages, and if you're balancing stones so that someone coming along after you will be able to find their way, then it's a good idea to position your stones so that they'll be able to withstand winds and weather. (Add a little concrete if you must.) But if you're balancing stones for the sake of concentrating and focusing your mind, then two stones will be plenty. Sometimes less is more, and sometimes less is less.

Regardless of how many stones you work with, you have to give your full energy to the one in your hand. You may have a dozen to balance, but the balancing can't happen until you attend to the one, fingering every dimple, considering every ridge and angle. From the one, you'll determine how to arrange the twelve. This is how to be faithful.

15

I'd glimpsed Vetiver several times that day. He looked perfectly at home at Raven Creek Center for Spiritual Enlightenment. Like me, he'd been given additional clothes from the Lost and Found, and he didn't appear to care a smidgen that the collar of his shirt had points that extended past his shoulders. Someone had loaned him a rake, and he'd become caretaker of the trails that led from the main lodge to the different cabins and campsites down the hill.

But that night after the movie—a strange little flick about tribal tattooing—I made my way to Campsite N alone. I couldn't find Vetiver anywhere.

I wasn't too keen on camping, but figured if the Locklears could handle it, so could I. Our housing wasn't exactly a tent. It was more like an outdoor room, with a raised wooden platform for a floor and heavy canvas tarp walls attached to a rustic frame of two-by-fours. There was room to stand up inside, and the bedrolls had been left for us on large benches that doubled as beds. There were no cooking facilities, since we were to eat our meals in the lodge, and no bathroom facilities, since we were to use the group bathhouse a little farther down the trail. But we had electricity, and there was even a space heater, though we didn't need it that first night.

I waited there for a while, thinking Vetiver might be in the bathhouse. When he didn't return, I started to worry. Maybe he'd gotten lost in the woods. Who knew what kinds of creatures he might encounter? I got myself so worked up that I was almost afraid to visit the bathhouse, but eventually my bladder bested my nerves. I went to bed remembering other nights when I'd spent my precious energy worrying over fools.

When Craig and I were newly married, he'd gone out fishing with his cousin Jimmy. They'd pulled the boat up on a barrier island and gone off exploring, and when they got back, the tide had risen and the boat had floated away. They stayed out there all night, standing up through high tide, trying not to get washed out to sea before the water receded. I'd already started thinking of myself as a widow by the time the Coast Guard found them and brought them to shore. Another time when *The Lady Renee*'s engine went dead and Craig's phone couldn't get a signal, he and his crew had drifted until somebody spotted them and towed them in. All that night I'd pictured Craig sunken and drowned, with crabs munching on his eyeballs. Then he came home laughing.

I rolled over and committed to sleep, remembering that Vetiver had taken care of himself perfectly fine without my assistance until a few days back. He could be sleeping at Campsite XYZ, for all I knew.

Some time after that, he stumbled in, cussing and grumbling.

I startled and sat upright. "What is it?" I asked.

"I need a goddamned drink," he said.

"Just go to sleep," I told him.

"Can't sleep," he said. "Not without a drink."

"Yes, you can," I said. "With any sort of addiction, there's a biochemical component and a *habit*. At the very least, you can control the habit."

"Well, I beg your damned pardon," Vetiver muttered and he made a production of taking off his shoes and arranging his covers. Then he rolled and he tumbled. He grunted and mully-grubbed until finally he said, "You don't even care."

"I care," I said. "But since you've made it this long without a drink, maybe you'll be okay if you go to sleep."

"You oughta help me out," he said. "Wasn't for you I'd be back home and could get a drink when I need one."

"What do you expect me to do?" I asked. "Hitchhike to the ABC store? I did you a favor bringing you here," and I dozed off, thinking it was true.

Since we didn't have a clock, I don't know how much time passed before I heard him leaving. He couldn't find the door flap at first and nearly took down the walls making his escape.

"Where are you going?" I called.

"Gotta find a goddamned drink," he said.

I guess he walked all night to get one. He wasn't at Tai Chi the next morning. Sure, I went to Tai Chi. I'd never done it before, but when I went to breakfast, I discovered that Tai Chi came first. So even though I felt like a nut, I joined the back row and mimicked everybody else's movements, and I did fine until they all turned 180 degrees, and I was suddenly in the front. Soon enough we did a quarter turn, and then I was just somewhere in the middle.

A natural healer so well-known that he has his own vitamin line gave a talk later that morning about the importance of raw foods, not just salads but also juice drinks. Some of the people around me were actually taking notes, so I borrowed a sheet of paper and took down helpful hints about the combinations of vegetables that break up kidney stones or decrease the acidity of the blood. I kept hoping this healer would mention something about the right combination to help alcoholics detoxify, but before he came to that part, Sister Esther tapped me on the shoulder and motioned me outside.

"I sent Vetiver down to the pond," she said.

"What pond?"

"Over that hill," she said, "Maybe a quarter mile beyond.

There's a no-alcohol policy here at Raven Creek," she explained. "But nothing to prevent him from drinking when he's off the grounds. The pond is just beyond the property line."

"But he needs to *stop* drinking," I said. "Shouldn't we lock him in a room with that natural healer and offer him some beet juice or something?"

"It's not our decision to make," Sister Esther told me.

So I went down to the pond to check on Vetiver. That's where I found him relaxing beneath a tree, a case of Colt 45 between his knees and a little stack of cans already piling up.

In my mind, he'd almost gone off alcohol cold turkey, so when I saw him like that, I wanted to beat the starch out of him. I could feel my blood pressure rising—up my neck, through my cheeks and ears. "Look at you!" I said, and of course I meant: Look at what you've done! Look at how you've fallen! But he heard something altogether different. "Yeah," he said. "Look at me now," like he was the Emperor of Boozers.

MEATY TIDBITS

It's natural to be disappointed when you see someone not living up to his potential. But you have to remember that your idea of another person's potential is different from the potential itself. If you're the parent of a child who doesn't perform well in math, for example, then it's fine to buy flashcards or hire a tutor. But you may also need to modify your thinking. If your child has basic skills, if he can balance a checkbook, that might be enough. He can use a calculator or an accountant for the rest. Instead of shaming him for his low math scores, praise him instead for how beautifully (or dutifully) he plays the clarinet.

Anybody can do Tai Chi. Learning the postures and moves improves your balance and clears your mind. I still practice the short form some mornings down by the harbor. When the captains of the charter boats shake their heads, I keep right on spreading my wings like a crane or shaking my mane like a wild horse. In Tai Chi, the front becomes the back and the back becomes the front. When you're in the back, follow the person in front of you. When you're in the front, look to the person beside you. If all else fails, make up a new move. Even the moves practiced in China for ten thousand years were new moves once. And who wouldn't appreciate the chance to embody a ghost crab running for its hole or an osprey diving for a croaker? You don't even have to be creative to make up new moves. Mimic whatever's going on in the natural world, and you, too, can be a Tai Chi queen.

16

"A body image workshop?" I asked Sister Esther. "I don't really want to go to that one. Can't I do some chakra healing instead?" (At that time, I still pronounced "chakra" the way it looks, with a "cha" as in "cha-cha" or "chocolate." Now I know to say "shock-ra.") But the chakra class was full. Besides that, Mrs. Locklear had specifically requested the body image workshop.

So that afternoon I joined an all-female group in one of the cabins near the lodge. The leader was a woman with brunette hair that curled to her waist and dramatic eye makeup that made her look like she'd spent some time at The House of the Rising Sun.

Thank God she didn't ask us to look at our cervixes—or hers. But she did have us take pieces of rope and, without measuring, cut off the lengths we thought we'd need to fit around our breasts, our waists, and our hips. Then we all had to do it—actually put the breast-sized rope around our breasts and notice how distorted our idea of our size really was. We laughed a lot during that part of the class. Only one woman cried—a gal who didn't realize her waist was bigger than her breasts until that very day, though how she could have missed it eclipses me.

When she paired us up, I was assigned to work with the

woman with braids who had befriended Vetiver the morning before. Her name was Flora, and her dog, a male, had to stay out on the porch and sleep during our class. Flora was shaped like a pumpkin, with little skinny legs that looked even bonier in her black stretch pants. She laughed a lot and didn't have any sorrow about her round belly. (In fact, during the earlier exercise when the distressed woman had cried over her waist size, Flora had assured her that big bellies bring luck if you rub them, and offered her own sizable tummy to the woman for a stroke.) Flora's scraggly gray braids came down over her shoulders and crooked into her armpits, and it seemed like she kept bits of nuts in her mouth all the time and moved them around the tops of her teeth with her tongue.

"Myrtle," she said. "Vetiver's friend. Pleased to meet you," and she shook my hand vigorously and invited me to stretch out on the big piece of paper on the floor. We had to draw the outlines of each other's bodies. "Relax," she said. "I don't bite."

But it was hard to relax with her standing over me, crouched above me. I wasn't used to being touched by people that way, and when she knelt beside me to trace the outline of my head, I had to make myself not pull my shoulder away from her leg. I could smell her. She smelled like moss. The whole thing made me tense, and I was glad when it was over. But when it was my turn to draw her outline, she joked about how I was drawing her aura, not her body. "Help me out," she said. "You can thin me down by bringing that crayon in a hair."

When we had outlined our bodies, we made a great ceremony of cutting them free from the paper. Then the leader led us in a meditation where we were supposed to feel the energies in our bodies and note the places where we had tingles or aches, places where our bodies felt anger or shame.

"Now sit quietly and let all your attention turn to the part of your body calling out most clearly," the leader said.

My hoo-hoo immediately warmed up and began to pulse.

"Let it tell you what it needs," she said, but I refused to

listen. I tried to concentrate on other parts of my body, safe parts, like my elbows. I tried to channel Mrs. Locklear, figuring her aches were probably more respectable than mine.

Then, when our eyes were open again, we were instructed to take the crayons and color in what we'd learned.

Around the room, people colored like maniacs. Grown women on their hands and knees with crayons on butcher paper. I'd never seen anything like it.

"What's the matter?" Flora asked. "Why aren't you doing it?" She was drawing grapes in the middle of her belly: brown vines, green leaves, purple and reddish globes. She was making a whole lush arbor.

But how could I color in my supersized lippy? Just thinking about it, I could feel it thick between my legs. I wanted to take the scissors and amputate the whole crotch out of my paper representation, and I almost did it, too. Then I realized that what I really wanted to get rid of wasn't that flap of skin as much as the constant, nagging feeling that I was deformed. I put the scissors down on my drawing, right where my coochie would be, and I took up a black crayon and outlined the scissors there between my legs. Then I colored the whole thing red.

"Powerful," said the leader. "Do you want to tell us about it?"

"No, thank you," I said.

She sent us out into the natural world for thirty minutes to collect things to use to decorate our bodies. We were turning our cut-outs into goddesses by then. We used paints and glitter and glue and herbs and berries and pine needles and acorns to decorate our paper shapes.

"If it would help you to undress and rid your own body of constraints, feel free to do that here. It's a safe space," the leader said.

Around the room, women began shucking their clothes. Soon I was watching bare-assed women finger painting, squirting glue, making crazy headdresses out of grass tufts and leaves.

It seemed that I was the only one in clothes, so finally I pulled off my shirt so I wouldn't stand out. It might surprise you to learn this, but I've always had great boobs. Even Craig would admit that. I have no issues with my boobs whatsoever. But I couldn't help laughing when I imagined Craig getting a glimpse of me now, all decked out in my patchwork skirt with my boobs flinging as I reached for the petals of pansies. I have to admit I was having a good time. We'd all donned ivy crowns by then. I didn't have that much to be self-conscious about. Some of the women had scars and little pouches of skin where you'd never expect. One woman had cross-eyed nipples, and she didn't seem to mind, so why should I?

We put on our clothes and broke for dinner, but afterwards we carried our cut-outs to the edges of a fire circle where someone had strung up a clothesline between two birch trees. We hung ourselves on the line there, then sat on rocks and told stories about our bodies.

You've heard the stories before. We heard from a woman who'd been flat-chested all her life, how she'd suffered changing for gym. We heard from a woman who'd had a breast reduction and now mourned that violence she'd inflicted on herself. Another woman claimed her breast reduction was the best decision she'd ever made. We heard from a dancer with arthritis who had smeared putty on the joints of her cut-out figure to represent the stiffness there. We heard stories of rape and betrayal. One woman went over to her cut-out body to kiss all her shame spots.

When it was Flora's turn—Flora with her grape clusters adorning her lucky belly—she told us she had tumors. Each grape represented a cancer cell, she said. She pointed out the big grapevine on her drawing and lifted her shirt to show us the scar I hadn't noticed before when we were all half-naked and crazy with our glitter and glue. She told us that with her first diagnosis, she'd had surgery and chemotherapy treatments, but when it recurred, she'd decided instead to let the tumors grow.

"Let them flourish like grapes," she said, and around the fire circle a few people whooped and clapped in support, but I was certainly not the only one who said nothing.

Was she out of her mind? Hadn't she ever seen anybody die from cancer? How could she not fight *cancer*?

I was so startled and even upset by Flora's presentation that when it was my turn and the leader said, "Tell us your story," it didn't seem like I had much to say.

"I recently made an appointment with a surgeon," I said. "I'm a little lopsided down there." Some of the women nodded and laughed, like maybe they had danglers, too. It didn't seem like a very big deal anymore, not given what I'd seen that day. Some people had hairy trails running from their belly buttons into their bushy little coochies. Some had legs that looked like monkeys, legs that had possibly never been shaven. Some of these women, it turned out, were married to men who were off in the woods mourning their lost foreskins. It occurred to me that if Craig attended a body-image workshop, he might stop all his teasing. "But I changed my mind," I said. "It's just some extra skin. I'm glad I didn't cut it off."

They clapped for me, and I clapped, too, thinking *Lordy, Lordy, Lordy.*

When we'd all had our turns, we stood around the fire for a while, hugging and visiting and recalling all that had happened that day. I imagined giving a body image workshop in our little town, maybe at the library or even in the church basement on nights when they weren't having Al-Anon, and I wondered if anybody besides Dottie would sign up.

I went by the bathhouse and took a long shower. I was gritty and itchy with bug bites and had patches of glue and pine sap on my hands and arms. It's a myth that spiritual retreat centers don't have hot water—or at least they had plenty of it in the bathhouse at Raven Creek. It felt good to clean up. But as I soaped my legs, I thought about my mother's legs, the broken veins behind her knees, all red and purple, and I wondered if they bothered her. As I washed between my thighs I couldn't help considering my mom's preoccupation with smelling bad. All my life she'd kept feminine hygiene washes on the shelf in her shower, right beside the shampoo and crème rinse. I knew so little about her body image—and what I did know was speculation. How could I know so much more about these Raven Creek women—strangers—than I knew about my own mother, and what did that *mean*?

When I got back to Campsite N that night, Vetiver was there, but so was Flora, sitting astraddle him, her silver braids bouncing behind her. The dog was in my bed, so I went back to the fire circle, where I found Sister Esther alone roasting marshmallows. She offered me one, and I took it. I was crying, but maybe she didn't notice. Maybe she wasn't such a great psychic after all.

"That was quite a phallus you made for yourself, kitten," she told me. "Impressive! Those scissors!" Her marshmallow caught on fire and she poofed it out.

"That wasn't a phallus," I said. My own marshmallow stuck to my fingers and lips.

"Are you sure?" she asked. "Do you need to be more cutting? Do you need to be more threatening?"

"No," I said. "That was an accident, really."

"There's no such thing as an accident," Sister Esther said, and she whispered, "Snip, snip, snip."

MEATY TIDBITS

Alcoholics and people with cancer can still have sexual intercourse, and if you happen to catch them at it by accident, you can still feel jealous, even if you're sorry about their addiction and disease. It isn't surprising that I felt upset when Flora stole Vetiver away from me. Even though I didn't want Vetiver in a sexual way, he'd been my primary companion during the most traumatic week of my life, and now another woman, a woman full of tumors, no less, had stepped into the central place in his life. Of course I was jealous.

There's very little correlation between the way a body looks and the way a body feels. You can have great boobs without having great boob sensations. Or maybe you just need the right mouth there. Apparently, you can be the hairiest woman in the Northern Hemisphere and feel fantastic about your body, or you can be waxed and slick all over and still feel ugly. We kid ourselves when we confuse appearance and desire. The next time you look at some beautiful body and think that person has it made, remember that you once had a beautiful body, too, and didn't even know it. Remember that compared to someone else, you have a beautiful body right this minute, and give it a little extra love.

17

At Raven Creek, people came and went. Some showed up to attend one-day workshops; others came to stay a month. Presenters would sometimes fly in, give their talks, and leave on the same day. Others arrived a week early, did yoga, studied animal tracks, participated in drumming circles—all before giving their own presentations. And at Raven Creek everybody—leaders and followers alike—pitched in with the upkeep and maintenance.

That's how it happened that one night I shared kitchen duty with a famous Buddhist nun. I knew her reputation from Dottie, who was always reading her books, listening to them in her car, trying to get me to listen, too. Naturally, this nun made me nervous. For one thing, she was famous. For another, she was Buddhist. On top of that, she had a crew cut, and where I come from, women don't parade around in crew cuts.

There were stacks and stacks of dirty dishes, and at first it seemed like an impossible chore. "Where do we even start?" I wondered, and of course I meant it rhetorically, but this nun answered: "Start where you are." So I took the first plate, scrubbed the crusted quinoa from the surface, and passed it to her to dry.

She was only staying at Raven Creek overnight because later in the week, she was scheduled to teach at a nearby summer institute where people came by the thousands to listen to Dharma talks and be mindful together. That's how I found out that Raven Creek was a rest-stop for gurus, spiritual leaders-in-training, and their guinea pigs. People came there for rejuvenation—and sometimes to test their new ideas before taking them public.

"It's a well-kept secret, Raven Creek. How did you find out about it?" she asked me.

"From the Locklears," I said. I wondered what Mrs. Locklear was up to that night, if she was on holiday in Prague or maybe in the leukemia ward of some hospital. "Do you know them?" I asked. "The Locklears?"

This nun shrugged, smiled, and kept right on with her drying.

I worried I was using too much water. How much water would Mrs. Locklear use? Would she run a sink full, dunk the cleaned dishes, and pass them on? Or would she keep a thin stream trickling from the faucet so fresh water rinsed each dish? I tried to figure out a way to switch jobs with the nun. If I were drying instead of washing, I wouldn't have to worry about water at all. I knew I shouldn't waste water— especially in front of a nun—but then my job was to get the dishes clean. It seemed like there was no right answer, and from that small conundrum, I began to dwell on similar impossible situations—like the one I was in with Craig.

To keep from thinking about it, I made small talk: "My friend Dottie got your last book on audio," I told this nun. "She's never gonna believe I met you." I handed her another cup to dry and didn't mention that Dottie had fallen asleep in the tanning booth listening to her latest and greatest. Maybe that was a good thing, right? Creating relaxation?

This Buddhist nun didn't talk much. She took each dish that I handed her and wiped it carefully, sometimes polishing with her cloth and sometimes simply dabbing the water away. It made me uncomfortable to be standing so close to her without talking. I could hear the sloshy water, the blurps as I submerged the cups, and it seemed a little too personal. No matter what words you speak, they're rarely as intimate as silence. So I asked her questions: "What kind of workshop will you be leading next week?"

It turned out to be a silent retreat.

"What do you do at a silent retreat?"

She mentioned the benefits of sitting in communal silence—waiting past the discomfort, quieting the mind, heightening other senses, experiencing the energy of other beings without commentary.

"Do people really pay money for that?" I asked. "I mean, how would you ever know if you got your money's worth?" She shrugged, so I asked her, "Does it bother you to be in here washing the dirty dishes when you're a renowned spiritual teacher?" Believe me, I know that was a dumb question. Sometimes people say that there's no such thing as a dumb question, but there are plenty.

"Washing the dishes is a spiritual activity," she said. "Does it bother you?"

"No," I said, "But I'm used to washing dishes."

"Then maybe you should acknowledge your spiritual expertise," she said. She wasn't being snarky, though. If Dottie'd said it, if Craig had said it, even if I'd said it, it might've seemed snide. It wasn't snide the way she said it.

"I've never met a Buddhist nun before," I admitted. "I've never met a Buddhist *period*." The only Buddhists I'd seen wore red robes and came to the United States to make designs in the sand. I figured they'd probably be good at balancing stones, too.

"And to think I've been here all along," she teased.

She didn't ask me anything about my religious background, but I started telling her about my church—I couldn't help myself—how I'd grown up there, attended Bible school there, married Craig in the old sanctuary, helped with fundraisers for the new sanctuary, sat Sunday after Sunday next to Craig's parents without ever really feeling the spirit of God. "Then one day," I told her, "when the preacher was asking for prayer requests and someone called out the name of a plumber in our area, this old woman who'd given heaps of money to the church's building fund said, 'Wait a minute, Preacher. Ain't he a nigger?'

"The preacher said, 'Yes, ma'am. He's a black man.'

"And she said, 'Niggers ought not be on our prayer list. They got their own prayer list.'"

I passed the nun the salad bowl, suds dripping down my arms, and told her, "At that moment, I felt God calling me. If I've ever been called by God, I was called on that day to stand up and say something, or to stand up and walk out, or to do *something*. I don't know what God wanted me to do, but I know I was called."

"So what did you do?" the nun asked.

"Nothing," I said.

I reached for another stack of sticky plates, and when I did, I knocked a measuring cup right off the counter. It bounced across the floor, and though it was made of a heavy plastic, it cracked.

"Shit," I said, then "oops," because I didn't think I should cuss in front of a famous Buddhist nun.

But this one had a playful side, a twinkle in her eye. She didn't get upset at all. She shrugged and said, "Things break," like it happened naturally. "Before you make too much meaning of not heeding that call," she said, "Ask yourself what you were being called to do. You think you were called to stand up, make a speech, or walk out. Maybe you were being called to wake up."

MEATY TIDBITS

You can't learn wisdom from a textbook. Wisdom is obvious and simple. That's why Jesus preferred hanging out with children and animals. That's why Buddhist monks spend all that time making designs in the sand or ringing bells and being wowed by their tinkles and gongs. That's why Henry David Thoreau, a man with a Harvard education, spent all that time loafing around his beloved pond, watching the tadpoles dart and dip. He didn't confuse wisdom with theory.

There are people who claim that if God calls and you don't listen, God will stop calling, will turn away and leave you alone in the dark. Not only is this unlikely, it's a snooty-ass assumption. How can any human know what God will or won't do? But we can wash the dishes, attend to the simplest things and treat them like they matter. We can be thankful the dishes are dirty, thankful we had food to heap on those plates. We can be conscious of the dirty thing made clean, ready to use again. We can be thankful for the water and for the rag that scours the grime. We can dry what's wet with care and attention, knowing the clean will be dirty, the dry will be wet, the full will be hungry, the hungry will be full, and if you miss a spot on your dish, it's no tragedy. You can clean it again tomorrow. There will be another chance.

18

The next night when everybody else was at a poetry reading in the lodge's main room, I slipped into the business office and called Craig collect. It was early enough that I knew he'd be awake, but I wasn't sure if he'd accept the charges.

I expected him to holler, but he didn't. He just said, "I got your e-mail. Were all them things you said true? About resigning from your marriage and everything?"

"Yes," I told him. I was still wearing my wedding rings at that time, the thin gold band and the little teardrop diamond I'd never liked. It had once belonged to his grandma so I felt obliged to wear it.

I twisted the first ring over my knuckle and was working on the second one when he said, "Why'd you do me like that, Myrtle? That was a terrible way to do me." His voice was way too quiet, like in the days after his daddy died, not the hard-grieving days but the ones after, when his feelings froze inside him. I wiggled my rings back down.

"It just happened," I said, and then we sat in silence, and I wished he'd holler, but he didn't. I wasn't sure what else to say, so I sat there fiddling with my rings and listening to Craig breathe.

"You can't resign," he said finally. "A marriage is different from a job."

"I know that," I said, and pulled the rings off completely. It was so quiet that I could hear the poet speaking at the microphone. I had my feet propped up on the desk, and I slipped my wedding rings onto my toes and studied them from a distance.

Outside, the poet finished, and everybody started clapping. "What's going on?" Craig said. "Where you at?"

"It's open-mic night," I told him.

"Damn, Myrtle," he said. He didn't like the arts much and had never attended a single school play or pageant with me. "I guess you're into rap music now—"

"Poetry," I replied. I wiggled my toes and tried to get the rings to do the Hula-Hoop.

"Huh," he said. "I reckon you want a divorce, then?"

I didn't know if I wanted a divorce or not. What I knew was that Craig and I had communication problems. Big ones.

Another poet had taken the stage by then, someone acting out a dramatic monologue about a shipwreck. We sat through most of that poem in silence. Who knows what Craig was doing? I was playing horseshoes with my rings, tossing them at my toes to see if I could catch them.

"Come on home and let's talk about it," Craig said. "We got a lot to work out, but we can't do it with you gone."

"I can't," I said.

"We'll getcha some help," he said. "Wayne Larrimore's wife went to a counselor, and now she's doing a lot better." Like it was all *my* problem.

I didn't say anything. In the other room, the waves were breaking over the boat, and I knew that soon everybody was going to drown.

"You still with Hellcat?" Craig asked. "I swear, Myrtle . . ."

"His name's Vetiver," I said. "And I'm not *with him* with him."

"Everybody thinks he's poling your hole," Craig said.

"Who thinks that?"

"Everybody. Is he poling your hole?"

"No!" I said—but then I wondered about denying it, whether Craig would think I wouldn't let him pole my hole because he was black, when really that wasn't the case. Or was it? "He's got a lady-friend," I said. "A real nice woman with cancer."

"Is she there with you too?"

"Yeah," I said. "She's here, but not *here* here."

"Anybody else with you I need to know about?"

"No," I said.

"Well that's a relief," he said, and we both chuckled.

It was awful and comforting to talk to Craig—at the exact same time. Like wearing his old dumb diamond, which I slipped back onto my thumb.

Years back, Craig asked me what I wanted for our tenth anniversary. I told him I wanted a jewel to wear in my belly button. I was in a sexy phase then, but I didn't even care what kind of jewel he picked. He could have given me a rhinestone ruby, and it would have been fine with me. Instead, he gave me diamond earrings, all wrapped up in a JC Penney box. Until then, I didn't even know JC Penney sold diamonds. I made a point of wearing those earrings sometimes when we went out to supper. I didn't want to hurt his feelings since he was trying so hard to do what husbands just *did*.

Then, on our twentieth anniversary, he gave me a diamond pendant on a delicate gold chain. It was almost identical to the one he'd given me a couple of years before for my fortieth birthday. He didn't even know he'd given me two. In some ways Craig tried so hard, and in other ways, he hardly tried. Sometimes it seemed like the things he did that aggravated me most also endeared him to me.

"I didn't figure you were leaving me for *him*, not really," Craig said.

"Why in the world not?"

"Well, my God, Myrtle, if you were gone leave me for

another man, you could do a little bit better than *that,* don't
you think?"

"Vetiver's a better man than you know," I said to Craig.
"You wouldn't be able to hold him in judgment if you really
knew him."

Outside, the audience applauded. I could hear Flora
whooping. I knew they were getting ready to write haikus as
a group, and I didn't want to miss it. I was trying to figure
out how to get off the phone when Craig muttered, "He's still
a nigger."

I got a chill all through me then. I wished I hadn't bothered
to call. I wished I had a Buddhist nun to break some dishes
with. I asked myself: "What would a Locklear do?"

"Listen," I told Craig. "If you ever want to be with me again,
you can't talk like that. You can't even *think* like that." And I
hung up on him. Click. I didn't have time for that nonsense.

MEATY TIDBITS

*We tend to think of rules as limitations, but sometimes
rules restrict us in order to free us. Consider writing
haikus. A haiku isn't a lesser poem because it's short.
The limit on the line length requires the poet to "go
vertical"—or so says Vetiver, who turned out to be
downright gifted with the form. Though he's become
skilled at free verse in recent months, Vetiver will attest
that it helps beginning poets to have simple rules to
follow, like with haikus, when you have to count your
syllables:*

> *The Crepe Myrtle tree*
> *Sheds her bark beneath the moon.*
> *Newborn comes the dawn.*

On the other hand, simply having a structure, a 5-7-5 syllable pattern or even one of the more complicated forms—the pantoum, villanelle, or sestina—doesn't necessarily make anyone a great poet. My own haiku went like this:

Flo and Vetiver
Sitting in a Tree. K I
S S I N G

Though Vetiver cheered when I read it, the poet-in-residence didn't ask me to take his workshop or sit at his table. I didn't get my feelings hurt because I don't have to be good at everything I try. Neither do you.

19

Later that week Sister Esther and I were weeding the herb garden. As we made our way through the basil and thyme, I ranted about Vetiver and how he continued to drink and about Flora who kept driving him into the nearest town to buy more alcohol. It turned out that Flora had her own car there—she'd been driving up to Raven Creek from her home in South Carolina each spring for the past five years—and so whenever Vetiver's stash got low, off they'd go, skipping out on the dream-work sessions or whatever opportunity they had. If they missed dinner, they didn't even care. They'd come back with Taco Bell. They were shameless about it, too. There I was, eating healthy vegetarian meals, breathing clean air, trying to find my spiritual center and make meaning out of the past weeks of my life, and there was Vetiver, enjoying a Nacho Gordita Crunch and stuffing his Lost and Found satchel with malt liquors to take down to the pond.

"She's enabling him," I tattled. "How can that be healthy?"

Sister Esther had a way of turning around everything I said. "He's enabling *her*," she countered. "Enabling her to forget her troubles. Enabling her to enjoy the moment. This word 'enable'—you speak it with such derision. Why is that?"

"Haven't you ever been to Al-Anon?" I asked.

"What does the word 'enable' mean to you, Myrtle?"

"It means she gives him power to make the mistakes he was already making before he came here." I caught myself before she had a chance to correct me about mistakes and rephrased: "She gives him power to continue drinking."

"Okay," Sister Esther said. "But there's a part of the meaning that you're overlooking. First, she 'gives him power.' So it's no surprise that Vetiver feels good when he's around Flora and prefers her company to yours. We all like to be given power and trusted with power. Giving others power is a way to love."

"But that's ridiculous!" I yanked up a whole clump of parsley and chucked it in the weed pile.

Sister Esther hushed me. "Would you prefer the rosemary or the chives, dear?" I took the chives and we continued our talk down the next row. "What would you say is the opposite of enabling?"

"Disabling, I guess," I said. "And if Flora's braids weren't so tight she might see that she'd be giving him more power if she took away his ability to get what he wants, since what he wants is a *known toxin* to him."

Sister Esther considered this. "Can you give me an example of how that's true in the natural world?"

"Jesus," I said. "Just forget it."

"Now I think we're getting somewhere," she said. "To enable is to assist. To help. To make what's difficult easier. Is anyone enabling you, kitten?"

Of course I began to cry. Looking back now I see that I was being enabled in every way. I was staying at Raven Creek for free, enabled by fate or God, the Locklears or Sister Esther (and maybe they were all the same thing anyway). Every breath I took had been given to me. I had food, a place to sleep, and I was being challenged, forced to question my every assumption. I realize now that being enabled is itself an act of grace, and Christ was and remains the consummate enabler. The enabling is separate from the action an enabled one takes.

But at that moment, I was overcome with self-pity. "Nobody

enables me," I said. "That's part of why I had to leave." I realized then how necessary my leaving was for my own survival. "I spend all my days in a classroom with the children other people have given up on, trying to enable *them*. I give them everything I've got, and nobody notices. I've never won teacher of the year," I said. "I've never even been nominated," and I cried into the chocolate mint.

"Go ahead, dear," Sister Esther encouraged.

"I get home from work and have to place the bait order for Craig. He could do it himself, but he doesn't like to talk on the phone, and his momma has a lisp. So I do it. I used to do it out of the goodness of my heart, and now it's become my job. Then I fix supper, and most times all I get in return is a big old burp."

"Well now," said Sister Esther, "a satisfied burp is a certain kind of thank you."

"I guess," I said. "More often than not I end up overcooking Craig's hamburger, and we get in a tiff about it. He'd eat it raw if I let him."

"Why don't you let him?" she asked.

"Bacteria!" I said. "E. coli!"

She tisked and smiled at me. "The chances are slim."

"Then in the nights, he wakes me up and wants . . . you know . . . And I'm *sleeping*. I'll be damned if I'm gonna enable him then!" I said.

"You feel like he doesn't respect you."

"I feel like a doormat," I said. "And the next morning he wakes up pouting. But I need my sleep because I have to go back into that classroom and try to raise the SOL scores for a group of children who can't pass the tests they have to take. They could pass *different* tests, mind you. They're not stupid—"

"It's no wonder you're so sad," Sister Esther said.

"I'm not sad," I said, snot dripping now onto the sage. "I'm raging!"

"Same thing," said Sister Esther.

"Saturdays and Sundays I either help out at the Crab Cribb

or scrub out that skanky old boat. I spend every summer working behind the counter because Craig and his momma are too cheap to hire a high school student who'd do it for minimum wage."

"So the life you've been living isn't the life you pictured," Sister Esther said.

"Not at all," I confessed. "And now Vetiver! Before I drove away with him in the back of my truck, he spent his days hoping somebody'd let him pull the poison ivy off the side of their barn and pay him ten dollars to do it! And I freed him. I got him away. Now he has this chance. He even has someone to love, which is a *lot* more than I have right now."

"In that case," Sister Esther said, "I think you should demand what you deserve."

Looking back on it now, I'm not even sure what Sister Esther meant by that comment. Should I demand to be paid for my work in the summers? Should I demand to be appreciated more by Craig? Or was what I deserved a thank you from Vetiver? With a year's distance, I can interpret her advice in so many ways. But back then I was more of a hothead, and I stomped right off, headed for that pond and for Vetiver, the thankless old lush.

MEATY TIDBITS

No matter what your life looks like, it won't be the life you pictured. The life you're living comes with ingrown toenails, heating systems that break down, and audits by the IRS. You didn't picture any of that, did you? Whatever life you imagine—whether you see yourself as a world-renowned medical researcher or a master chef— you'll imagine without pain or worry. You'll never have shingles or jury duty in your fantasy life. But we need the space between reality and fantasy. It reflects back to us our youth.

There's nothing you can do to help an alcoholic or drug addict, no matter how much you may want to. Short of a conversion experience (which, by the way, you can't provide), the addict will continue to destruct. But if you have an addict in your life, you can do something for yourself. You can free yourself of the illusion that you have the power to make any difference in regard to the addict's addiction. You can love the addict best by loving yourself, concentrating on your own growth, working toward your own spiritual awakening.

20

The walk to the pond was uphill, then downhill, and the trees stretched with new branches that I had to push aside. On the descent, there were slippery spots where I had to step carefully and grab onto everything from vines to the ground itself to keep from sliding down. I was out of breath by the time I spotted Vetiver sitting on a flat rock near the water. He waved and pointed out a turtle on a nearby log. "That old cooter was just about to jump," Vetiver said. "But you scared him."

Another accusation! I'd ruined it for his damned old turtle. I made my way down there in a huff and plopped down on the boulder beside him. I didn't even know what I wanted to say. Vetiver's cigarettes were sitting there in his shadow, and I leaned over and helped myself to one, figuring that ought to get his attention. I lit it, nasty old thing that it was, and I puffed away as we watched that turtle. Vetiver didn't seem to care a bit. It didn't even register that I'm not a smoker.

"He'll jump," Vetiver promised, like he thought I was holding my breath for the magic turtle moment. "Just wait."

Vetiver's satchel of Colt 45s was one rock higher up and in the shade. He wasn't even drinking. I tore into it and helped myself to a hot can of malt liquor. Again, no reaction. He looked at that turtle and relaxed in the breeze. I tried to make small talk, but Vetiver just said, "Mh-hmm. Mh-hmm."

The old turtle would raise his head and look around, then take a step and crouch back down.

I wish I could have quieted my mind, but my mind didn't work like that. To tell the truth, most times it still doesn't. It seemed like everybody else at Raven Creek, Vetiver included, could relax and appreciate being out on a rock, feeling the sunshine on their heads. I told myself maybe my problem was biochemical. Maybe I needed a prescription drug to calm me. Several days before a doctor had given a breathing demonstration to teach us how to breathe, counting on the inhale, holding it for bit, then exhaling slowly, getting rid of every last bit of air in our lungs and making it take a long time. Whenever we were stressed, we were encouraged to breathe like this five or six times, then return to regular breathing. Sitting there with Vetiver and the old turtle, I did my breathing exercise, and when it was over, I was so dizzy it's a wonder I didn't fall out. Again, Vetiver didn't notice.

"I got one for you," he said, and then he recited:

Cooter on a log
Dried out shell and pruned up neck
Water just below

"Your turn," he said.

Like I'd hiked all that way to dream up turtle poems. I was almost sure that if I were Flora, he wouldn't be spending his time making up haikus!

So I peeled off my shirt. Vetiver glanced over at me, startled, then turned right back to the turtle. Like I'd hurt his eyes.

So I took off my long patchwork skirt. I kicked off my underpants and made a production of rolling all my clothes up together into a pillow I could lean against. Then I stretched out on my back and let my supersized labia warm there next to Vetiver in the sunshine.

Vetiver glimpsed my way, and then shifted his whole body so his back was to me. "What's the matter with you?" he asked. There was more than a little bit of a scold in his voice.

"Nothing's the matter with me. What's the matter with *you?*"

"I'll tell you what's the matter with me," he said. "You're playing with my head, and I don't appreciate it. Put your clothes back on."

"You think I'm undressing for you?" I said. "Ha! I'm doing it for that turtle." And I tried to think up a haiku about it, but wasn't fast enough.

Vetiver stood up to leave. "What do you want from me?" he asked.

What *did* I want? I wasn't even sure – but it was too late to back down. "I wanna be seen," I said.

"I see you," he replied. "Now put your clothes on."

"No," I said. "I don't feel like it."

He started stomping away, leaving both his malt liquor and his cigarettes. I couldn't let him do that. So I jumped up quick, ran up behind him, and shoved him into the pond.

I'd done it before I even realized I was about to. He stumbled and then splashed sideways into the water, startling the turtle on the log. The turtle went under and so did Vetiver, and the dark water closed over them both. When he didn't come right up, I jumped in, too, thinking I'd killed him. But the pond was shallow, and Vetiver emerged a little farther down, coughing and sputtering. He had green algae clinging to his head, and he took a big handful and slung it at me. It slapped me right in the face.

"Bitch," he said.

"I'm sorry," I said, and I reached out my hand, but he turned away and started dragging himself out and up the bank. When his footing was steady, he pulled off more strings of algae and pelted them my way. He gathered my clothes and threw them down to me where they floated on the algae screen.

"It's time for you to go home to your husband," Vetiver shouted.

"He doesn't respect me," I hollered back.

"That's probably 'cause you don't respect yourself," he said.

"Don't you try to shame me," I said. I retrieved my clothes but didn't put them on right away. Murky slime slooshed up between my toes.

Vetiver stormed over the rocks, slipping and dripping, and I watched him go. But when he got to the top of the hill, he turned back. "You don't want me, woman," he said. "Only reason you're stripping in front of me is 'cause you got a story in your head, and you don't know how to end it. Just cause we come all this way together don't mean something *else* is supposed to happen."

"What are you talking about?" I wiggled into my T-shirt.

He shook his head. "You know what? I feel sorry for you," he said. "You're miserable 90 percent of the time. You're so stuck in your own shit that you can't see anything else."

"I'm not miserable," I said. "I'm scared," and it surprised me to hear it. I hadn't really realized I felt scared until right that minute.

"Everybody's scared," he said, softer now. "It's perfectly normal to be scared, but that's no excuse to show your ass. You got it made, Myrtle Cribb." He stretched out both his arms like he was hugging the wind. "Look at this world you're a part of," he said. "Just look at it."

MEATY TIDBITS

When you find yourself engaged in a drama, don't assume you're necessarily the star. Often in my own life, I take for granted that I'm playing the lead. If I imagine myself acting out one of the classic epics, I'm Odysseus, not the singing vampire who tries to seduce him. If I imagine myself in the wilderness for forty days and nights, I picture myself in the role of Jesus, not Satan. It was only after I stripped naked at the pond and then shoved Vetiver into the water that I realized I'm sometimes Satan. Sometimes I'm not the main character at all, but the antagonist in someone else's drama.

If you ever push somebody into a pond and get a slimy wad of algae chucked in your face, don't be too quick about saying "Ooh, nasty!" Algae produces the oxygen we breathe and serves as an ingredient in many life-saving medications. If you're hard-up and hungry, it's chock-full of protein. So look past the ick factor and recognize the divine force dwelling there. At the same time, an overgrowth of algae can kill off fish, contaminate drinking water, and infect you with itches and boils and the runs. Like the algae, we, too, contain the capacity to bring goodness and harm to others. Whether we're at our best or at our most destructive, we're still manifestations of the divinity of the universe.

21

Vetiver hadn't slept at Campsite N since our second night at Raven Creek, so it was no surprise that he wasn't there when I returned to camp. I was feeling particularly lousy about myself when I went to the bathhouse to clean up. That's where I crossed paths with Flora.

I was already in the shower when she shuffled in, but she yoo-hooed and took the stall beside me. Though I expected Vetiver had told her what had happened at the pond, she didn't seem mad. In fact, she warned me to be careful not to slip when I left. Her dog had been drinking from the toilet again, and he'd dribbled all over the floor tiles.

I finished my shower before she did, dried off, and dressed. Her dog trotted over to see me, and when I rubbed his head, I felt a lump on his ear. I ran my thumb over it to push past his hair and discovered a big, fat tick.

"Flora," I called. "Your dog has a tick on his ear."

"Okay," she said.

"You better get it off."

The old spigot squealed as she turned it. "It's all right," said Flora. "That tick lives there on my dog."

I thought she might be teasing, but soon realized that she probably didn't understand. "It's a tick," I said. "Ticks carry Lyme Disease and Rocky Mountain Spotted Fever."

"Some do," she said. "Some don't." I heard her squeeze the water from her braids in short twin splats.

"But just in case," I said.

"Some people carry diseases, too, but we don't kick them out of their homes for it." She emerged from the shower stall wrapped in a too-small towel that gaped at her tumor-filled tummy.

"Maybe that tick's what's making your dog so sluggish," I said.

"My dog's sluggish because he's old," she replied.

"But what about animal cruelty?" I wondered.

"Cruelty to whom?" she asked. "The dog or the tick?"

I felt a little lightheaded. Confusion does that to me sometimes.

Flora added, "For all we know, that dog and that tick might be best friends."

I patted the dog's head—and I guess I patted the tick's head too. The dog looked sleepy and pleased. I smiled at Flora and she smiled at me.

"For all we know," she said, "that tick might be singing lullabies in the dog's ear even as we speak."

MEATY TIDBITS

Some people see cancer cells as invaders, as a colonizing evil. Obviously these people believe cancer should be eradicated. Others see cancer cells as the deviant children of hardworking parent cells. These people think the cancer cells must be rehabilitated and tamed. A third group maintains that cancer cells are parasites. These folks don't believe the cancer is bad in itself or bad for doing what cancer naturally does. If you get a person with each of these beliefs together in a room, you'll be looking for the back door directly because the conversation will become intolerable. Each person's view will dictate the way she lives and behaves, so certainly she must invest completely in it. But here's the kicker: the same God in the cancer cell exists in the non-cancerous cell. When the body decays, the God energy does not. So from a collective perspective, it doesn't make any difference how we categorize cancer or whether or how we treat it.

Sometimes when you're being your biggest and best self, someone else will see you as the cancer. And you are *the cancer, as far as that other person is concerned.*

22

I couldn't sleep that night. I wanted forgiveness from everyone I'd harmed, but I wanted it right that minute and didn't know how to make that happen. I took a late night walk around Raven Creek, past the fire pit, where some people were still drumming and smudging and dancing in the dark, past the empty cabins where workshops were held, past the occupied cabins where lights were dim. A few people waved to me from porches. A couple invited me out into a clearing to watch the stars, but I said no, that I needed to be alone.

Somehow I knew it was true. I needed to be alone, but I hated to be alone. And I was more alone than ever. I didn't have Craig anymore. I didn't have Dottie. I hadn't even talked with my parents, although I really needed to do that. Now I'd alienated Vetiver, too. There was so much I needed to fix. I walked all the way down the trail and out to the parking lot, where I found Flora and Vetiver in the car, smoking clove cigarettes and listening to music. The dog and his tick were crashed out in the backseat.

"Hop in," Vetiver said. He didn't mention anything about what had happened at the pond.

"I shouldn't," I said.

"Oh, come on," Flora urged, and told the dog to move over. So I did.

"Let's play it again for Myrtle," said Vetiver. "Listen to this," and he hit the back button on the stereo. The singer was some Celtic woman who wailed out a long and yearning poem by a famous long-dead Lord. The music interpreted the emotion of the poem so completely, with such high callings and such low laments, that it left me tingling and wanting something I couldn't name. There was one point in the song where even the dog cried—maybe because it got a little shrill. They passed the cigarette back to me, but I waved it away. I was having a hard enough time getting my breath.

After a while I left them there. Vetiver said, "Sleep good," and I said, "You, too," and that was the extent of our conversation and the occasion of our truce.

Back at Campsite N, once again I tried to sleep, but I had voices in my head—Vetiver's, Flora's, Sister Esther's, the voices of so many people I hardly knew. I couldn't stop them, and I wondered if I could be high from breathing in secondhand clove smoke. I was lying there counting my breaths when something crashed. It sounded like someone had tripped over the fan. I jerked upright. "Who's there?" I asked. "Vetiver?" But no one answered.

When my eyes adjusted, I could see a dark shape on the floor, a figure crouching at the end of Vetiver's bed. I wondered if it might be a Locklear.

"Get out," I said. I couldn't decide whether to turn on the lamp. Did I want to see? The lamp was my only weapon, so I picked it up by the base to warn the intruder, and then I flicked it on.

At that very moment, the red fox pounced, leaping up in the air and right for me. I don't know if I dropped the lamp or if the impact knocked it from my hands. The fox landed on my chest, and though she didn't weigh very much at all—probably no more than my cat Purvis—she knocked the breath right out of me. I could feel her claws digging into my ribs and clinging to the tops of my thighs where my legs met my torso.

Somehow I knew enough to be very, very still. My only light was broken, and now I'm sorry I didn't get a better look at the particulars of the fox's pointed little face. "Easy," I said, maybe to myself. "Easy."

We stayed that way for a while. Me on my back, peeking over my own nose at the fox on my chest. I kept my eyes open, locked with her eyes, and the darkness made this tolerable. I was terrified, of course, but I kept saying to myself, "You and this fox were cut from the same divine fabric," and it didn't sound hokey then at all. The fox hadn't bitten me, and she'd had ample opportunity. My worst wound might be scratches from her landing.

The fox sat down on my chest. Though she was slight, her weight was hot and palpable. I knew that if I breathed slowly, there'd be no sudden moves, so I counted my breaths. Five times I did the calm breathing exercise, and still the fox didn't budge.

So I whispered, "What do you want, Red Fox?"

She replied, "I was hunting. I thought I smelled a mouse in here."

I wasn't expecting her to answer, of course, but I kept very still. "I think I might be having a nervous breakdown," I confessed. (I'd always pictured a crack-up as a messy, snotty enterprise. This was a calmer sort.)

The fox said, "A breakdown is nothing to be nervous about. When you break down, you get to put everything back together again. How will you arrange your life this time?" This fox talked a lot like Sister Esther.

"I don't know," I said. "For a long time I've felt so trapped."

"Then take advice from me," she said. "You have to outsmart the ones who try to trap you. When you see a trap, spray your urine in that direction and run the other way."

"Oh," I said. "Okay."

I could sense myself relaxing beneath her, giving in to her. In fact, I had to work hard not to laugh when I pictured myself pushing out my hips and spraying pee at the door of the Crab Cribb, where I did not want to spend any more summers selling crabmeat, lugging around coolers full of ice, wrapping fish filets in newspaper. I closed my eyes and remembered what it felt like to have Purvis climb onto me while I slept. I could almost hear her purring and wondered if the red fox also purred.

Then a thought so silly struck me that I giggled outright. "Care to share?" asked the fox, and I told her I'd have to spray my urine at the church door the next time they asked me to run the nursery. Everybody there thought I should want a baby and hoped if they assigned me nursery duty long enough, I'd get busy making one. The closer I got to menopause, the more nursery duty I was assigned. (Nobody knew about Craig's sluggish sperm. He made me promise not to tell. Instead, I was supposed to say: "I know that children are gifts from God, but I'll take my gifts from 8-3, with a school nurse and principal available for emergencies, and with summers and holidays off.")

"You should do it," the fox said. "Spray it up as high as you can."

"I don't go to that church anymore," I explained. "I ran away."

"Well, when you go back," the red fox said. "Even if you've been away from your den for months, you can return. Your den is your den," she said. "If a badger tries to claim it, you can run it off."

"Okay," I said, wondering if any badgers had snuggled in the sack with Craig. "I'll remember that."

"Whenever you feel stuck, call on your fox energy. Fox energy makes you witty and quick," she said. "Self-sufficient and wily."

"But I'm not a fox," I said. "And besides that, I'm middle-aged and tired. I never meant to be so slow and middle-aged and tired."

"That's why I'm here," said the red fox. "I came to pounce on the mouse in you!" At that, the fox flexed, pushed off, and bolted out of the room. I jerked upright on my bed, realizing I'd almost fallen asleep. How could I have slept with a fox on my chest?

I'd grown so warm that I was sweating—or maybe the fox had been sweating. I felt almost like she'd seeped into me. And the dreams I had—oh, but those are private. When your own spirit animal comes to you, you'll most certainly understand.

MEATY TIDBITS

Whether you know it or not, you exude energy constantly, and your energy changes the beings around you. Your fox energy will cause people to react to you in one way; your badger energy will cause them to behave in another. If you don't like the way you're being treated, check to see what kind of vibe you're giving off.

Where you spend your time isn't just the backdrop for your days. Places have power. Paddling a kayak through marsh grasses can bring serenity. Visiting your cousin at the jailhouse can make you grit your teeth. One school year on our annual trip to Jamestown with the fourth graders, we took the ferry across the river and stopped by Bacon's Castle, a place where slaves were whipped so mercilessly that blood still stains the old wooden floor. All the way home, those children were riled up, angry, and sorrowful. Places change people. Hang out too long at the insane asylum and soon you'll be running down the hall swinging a pool cue at the psychiatrist. But by the same token, you can live in a shack and be happy if you fill it with flowers. When you go to a place where there's been great openness and love, even generations before, you can be uplifted. So I recommend marshes over jailhouses, rooms full of flowers over castles full of blood. Even if you aren't a full-blown spiritual seeker, I recommend a spiritual place, every now and then, or maybe a cozy foxhole.

23

The next morning at yoga, Sister Esther could tell that something extraordinary had happened inside me. I was light on my feet, she said, and more flexible than she'd seen me before. She beamed at me and told me it was time to begin thinking about my own calling. What dreams had I not yet fulfilled? What stones had I not yet turned over?

"I don't know," I said.

"Of course you don't," she comforted. "But the time has come to ponder these questions."

I worried she might send me off into the wilderness on a vision quest. Instead, she sent me packing. Our time was up. The Locklears had only paid for ten days at Raven Creek.

"You're kidding," I said. "Why didn't you tell me sooner?"

Sister Esther said, "I assumed you knew!" She thought it was funny. She laughed and said, "You must have needed to *not* know."

Check-out was at eleven. Someone else would be occupying Campsite N that very night.

"But I wanted to walk the labyrinth," I protested. We'd been planning the labyrinth for days, going over designs with Carl, who was in charge of mowing the tall grasses in an overgrown field so that spiritual seekers could follow the path to their centers. Sister Esther had even suggested that we sprinkle wildflowers along the labyrinth walls so that later in the summer, surprises of all sorts would bloom there.

"You *will* walk the labyrinth," Sister Esther reassured. "The true labyrinth. The one at the Department of Motor Vehicles when you need new license plates. The one at the shopping mall, when it's Christmas and there's nowhere to park your car. You'll walk the labyrinth a thousand times."

"So that's it?" I asked.

"Kitten," she purred. "You're ready."

It turned out that Vetiver *wasn't* ready—not ready to leave Flora, anyway, and since they were sharing a bed, he wasn't costing Raven Creek a dime. By doing trail maintenance each morning and trash collection each evening, he was more than paying for his meals. Flora'd rented a private cabin and had it for another week. Before I left, she drew me a map to her farm down in South Carolina. "There's a hide-a-key in the shed beneath the purple paint can," she said. "If things don't work out with Craig, let yourself in."

It all happened so fast I didn't have time to process it. I checked in my bedroll and sleeping bag, returned the patchwork skirt and T-shirts to the Lost and Found. My new friends walked me out to the parking lot and hugged me goodbye. "The schedule for next year will be online in February," Sister Esther said. "Sign up early."

Since Flora was feeling weak and needed a nap, Vetiver drove me to the airport in her car. The dog and his tick rode along. I was glad he played the radio on the first part of the drive. I was sad to leave him and didn't really want to talk. As we crossed the mountain and made our way along the state road, my sadness turned into something else—I was miffed—and by the time we merged onto the highway, I was outraged. Why hadn't anyone told me my days were numbered? I needed time to psychologically prepare. Since no one else was there to fuss at, I took it out on Vetiver.

"Hold on a minute," he said. "Time to *psychologically*

prepare? Let me ask you something. What made you feel so secure in the first place? How come you feel like you were owed more than you got?"

"That's not what I meant."

"That's what you said," Vetiver replied. "You reckon Craig Cribb thinks he deserved a chance to *psychologically prepare* for your leaving?"

"I had a good reason," I said.

"I doubt it looked that way to him. You reckon those children you teach felt like they deserved a chance to *psychologically prepare?*"

"Quit mocking me," I said. "You're being mean. You know I didn't intend to hurt them."

"Most times people don't," Vetiver said. "Most times people do the very best they know." He lit up a cigarette and cracked his window for the smoke. "I'm not saying you did wrong, Myrtle. I'm just suggesting nobody else necessarily did wrong either."

So I dropped it. In my mind, I made plans. I'd fly back to the city where I'd left my truck, take a cab from the airport to the train station, pay my parking fee, and then once I had the truck back, I'd find a place to stay for the night. I was perfectly capable of going the rest of the way alone—but just because I was *able* didn't mean I *wanted to.* A hard swallow swelled up in my throat. I turned my face toward the window so Vetiver wouldn't see me cry.

I don't know whether or not he noticed. In a little while, he said, "We had us a trip, then, didn't we?"

"Sure did," I said. Then we were both laughing, hard, and then I was crying outright, and Vetiver reached over and gave me three sweet pats on the thigh.

"Not gon' be the same without you," he said.

"You know where you're headed next?"

"Down to South Carolina, I figure. Help Flora out, assuming she'll have me."

"I don't think you have to worry about that," I said.

"You never know," he said. "She's the proud type. Likes her independence. Likes to do things her way."

We were almost to the airport when we passed a sign for a waffle house. Even though I wasn't hungry, I talked Vetiver into stopping. I didn't actually have a plane to catch. I hadn't even bought a ticket. Clearly I was stalling, but under the circumstances, eating breakfast for the second time that day made perfect sense.

I was stirring around in my eggs by the time he confessed that he was seriously worried about Flora's health. "She says she's not hurting, but she moans in her sleep," he said. "A lot."

"Is she on medications?"

"Vitamins and garlic. She's starting the *macrobionic* diet, whatever that is," he said. "Says she's gonna teach me to cook seaweed."

"Ugh."

"I know it," he said. He blew out a sigh, a big one. "Whew, Lordy, Myrtle. You know, she's gonna die—" He held that syllable long and high, "die." Then he looked down at his plate and shoveled up a bite of pancakes. He stuffed it in his mouth and chewed and chewed and chewed. I thought for sure he was going to have to spit it back into his napkin.

His water glass was empty, so I passed him mine. "We're all gonna die," I said.

He took a big gulp and thanked me with his eyes. "But Flora's gonna die sooner than most," he whispered.

"We don't know that. Not really."

"She is. Unless we talk her into treatments. You reckon we should try to talk her into the treatments?"

I shook my head. "The reason she likes being at Raven Creek so much is because nobody tells her what to do."

Vetiver nodded. A single tear ran down beside his nose, plopped off his chin, and landed in the butter on his pancakes. "I can't do this," he said. "I can't lose another one."

"You can do whatever you have to," I said.

We sat together in silence for a while, and I fought off the urge to chatter. Even now, knowing that my chatter is a nervous behavior, I sometimes slip into it, commenting on the most meaningless observations or else giving unwanted advice. But every now and then, like on that day at the waffle house, I pretend to be a Buddhist nun and hold it.

"There was this one time," Vetiver told me. "I was a boy. Had an old bulldog I loved. Hadn't never had shots or nothing. Ate table scraps and slept under the porch."

He was whispering, and I could hardly hear him. I had to listen past the clinking forks and the buffet bar where someone was scraping the bottom of the oatmeal pot.

"I knew the dog had worms, but back then all dogs had worms. Didn't know they could kill a dog. One day I called him, and he didn't come. I looked around 'til I found him back behind the barn, laid out on his side, panting. I wrapped him up in a tobacco sheet, carried him like a baby home to my momma. He was a big old heavy thing, too. Didn't even fight me to tote him like that. His eyes were rolled back, tongue sticking out. Momma said it was too late, and I sat on the back doorsteps holding that dog like a baby, just a-crying."

Vetiver sniffed. "Then I noticed these little ripples under his skin. I put my hand on his belly, and you could feel 'em writhing in there, the worms. Felt like they were rearing up and rolling over one another. Sickest thing you ever felt. I jumped up, and when I did, I heaved that dog right into the bushes. It was like one motion, jumping up and throwing that dog."

I put down my fork, knowing I wouldn't need it anymore.

"Can you believe that? Probably the last thing that dog remembers is landing in the azaleas. I can still hear the thud. Knocked the wind right out of him. He let out a groan, sorrowful as you ever heard, and then he died." Vetiver looked me hard in the eyes. "So you tell me, how in the hell am I gonna take care of Flora?"

It was all I could do not to turn away. "You just will," I said. "You just will."

Vetiver went to the bathroom and stayed gone a while. When he came back, he'd washed his face. His whole attitude was different. He'd switched into fatherly mode. We were clearly done with all talk about Flora. "Now when you get back home," he coached, "don't act all ashamed. You hold your head up. Act like you *are* somebody."

"I plan to," I said.

"There'll be people who give you a hard time," he warned. "Don't listen to 'em. Don't give their words a bit of power."

"Gotcha," I said. I sent money with the waitress, left the tip beneath the syrup, and we headed back to the car. The rest of the way to the airport, I fed Flora's dog little bits of ham I'd wrapped up in a napkin.

We followed the signs for "Departures." Vetiver pulled over to the curb where you weren't allowed to park, and I knew I needed to hurry so that other passengers being dropped off could move into our space. But I didn't want to get out of that car.

"Listen," Vetiver said. "About Craig Cribb—try to give the man a chance."

I cut my eyes at him.

"I'm not saying you need to go back to the way things were, or even that you and Craig Cribb need to wind up together. I'm just saying, don't throw it away too soon. Sure as you can fall outta love with somebody, you can fall back in."

"You think?"

He shrugged. "Why not?" he said. "You got choices. Life's nothing but a big old maze, and you get to pick which way to go. One decision leads to the next, but there's not really a right or a wrong. If you run into a wall, just turn around and try again. You gotta keep on making turns, anyway, 'til you finally drop dead. Then you get to quit."

"You could write a poem about that," I suggested.

"Nah," he replied. "Can't say that kind of shit in a poem. Too heavy-handed."

I leaned over to hug him goodbye and he kissed me right on the nose.

MEATY TIDBITS

One of humankind's great faults is that we underestimate ourselves, assuming we're weaker than we actually are. When we hear stories about mothers who lift flipped-over four-wheelers off the bodies of children, when we hear about hikers trapped in the mountains who amputate their own limbs to save their lives, we think these things extraordinary. But we're all capable of things beyond our imaginations. People who go to the gym will have the tiniest inkling of this principle. When athletes think they can't do another repetition, another lap, they simply go one more, and then one more. What's true for our physical bodies is also true psychologically. Our limits are in our heads. We can push beyond them.

Be careful about who you surround yourself with. The people around you will either encourage you to be your biggest self or discourage you from trying. Spend time with the people who expect you to do better and be more.

ACTIVITIES FOR
FURTHER GROWTH

» Go to the supermarket produce section, and hang out discreetly with your eye on the salad bar. If you have a grocery list handy, take notes about the people who eat the berries or squares of cheese without paying. You may be surprised by what you learn. On the day I got drunk with Vetiver on the Amtrak, he told me the story of one of his arrests when he'd been caught stealing grapes from the salad bar and carted off to jail. When he asked if I'd ever sampled anything, I had to admit that I had. Many women I know nibble from the salad bar, and our preacher's wife has been known to graze there like she's at a cocktail party. To my knowledge, no one has ever arrested her for it. See if anyone is arrested while you're at the supermarket. Note whether they are neatly dressed or raggedy, whether they are white, Latino, Asian, Middle Eastern, or black. Note whether they seem hungry. Note reactions of any supermarket workers or managers.

» Study the lines on your hands and see if you can find a pattern there to suggest a new hobby or talent for yourself. You don't need to know what the lines actually mean to do this. If you see chicken scratches in your palm, consider if you want to raise biddies. If you see a Chinese design, maybe you want to learn a new language with a different kind of alphabet. Too many times when we look at the lines on our hands, we are dependent on fortune-tellers to interpret them for us. You can be your own fortune-teller. If you've ever seen shapes in the clouds, then surely you can see some in your own fingertips. Sometimes when you think you're making things up, you're actually tapping into deep-rooted, unconscious desires. Read the palms of everyone you know. Suggest to them talents and interests they haven't yet discovered.

» Make an inventory of your finances. Where do you bank? Invest? Who has access to your money? Regardless of your situation—whether you're male or female, married or single, regardless of your sexual preference, skin tone, or income—get your own bank account. Make sure your credit cards are in your own name. One day you might need to be able to buy something without your husband, wife, or otherwise beloved knowing it. One day, for reasons you can't even fathom, you might need to leave. Even if that day never comes, you ought to have the option. Don't forget: you can be committed to another person without sharing every penny you make or explaining where it went.

» If you and your husband, wife, or otherwise beloved fall into a season when you're no longer sexually compatible, consider whether you've unknowingly imbued your genitals with hurtful energy. Do this without blame. You aren't a true sadist just because you secretly picture for yourself a penis or vagina made of weaponry. But it could be that unconscious associations are interfering with your love life. In this case, I recommend a healing ritual. First, burn some sage and puff the smoke over your privates to smudge out negative energies. Next, break open the arm of an aloe plant and smear the juices over your skin. As you massage yourself, apologize for the wrongs you've committed against this sacred part of your body. (A warning: If you expect this ritual to later lead to oral pleasure, skip the aloe. It's bitter.) Feel the loving kindness warm you there. If negative thoughts or memories come up as you do this, acknowledge them, and picture them boarding a bus, one by one, and being driven away to rehab. Wave goodbye and allow other, happier images to take their place.

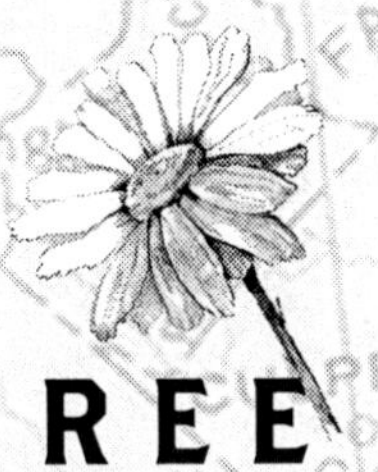

PART THREE

24

If you've ever watched an osprey fishing, then you've seen the way it soars high above the water. When it spots a fish, it hovers there, calibrates the distance, and then dives down quick, snaps up that fish, and zips to air where it does this flappy little wing dance as it gobbles and swallows.

Now imagine that you're an osprey out in your nest on the channel marker, and you're watching your mate go fishing. And suddenly, it drives you crazy how he flaps his wings when he's swallowing. Maybe you used to think it was cute, and now it looks ridiculous, and you know that the people on the pier with binoculars are pointing and laughing. Maybe all this time you've been fine with your mate flying off for twenty-minute stretches, but now you want your chance to go fishing sooner. You're aggravated with him for doing exactly what he's always done.

You might think you need a new nest all to yourself. Or you might think you need a new mate. Both those things could be true. But it might also be enough to renegotiate the terms of your relationship.

As I waited at the airport for my southbound flight, I found myself thinking about the big osprey nest out in the harbor. Craig and I had watched it, year after year. The same ospreys came back each spring. Supposedly ospreys mate for life, but who knows what they do in the off-season.

Somehow my parents had managed to stay together through all the ups and downs. They were overdue a phone call, and though I dreaded it, I worked up my nerve and found a pay phone.

"Oh, honey," my mother said. "We've been so worried. We got your postcard, but kept expecting you to call."

"I'm sorry," I said. "I needed some time to think. How was your cruise?"

She ignored me completely. "Well, Craig's a wreck," Mom said. "He was here when we got off the ship. Like to scared us both to death until we got the mail and saw that you were okay."

"You're kidding. Craig drove to Tampa? At the beginning of crab season?"

"He didn't stay but the one night. He's in bad shape, Myrtle, but if you don't love him anymore, then I guess you shouldn't go back home."

"I *do* love him," I said. "Did he tell you I didn't love him? That's not the problem."

Mom sucked in her air. "Well, what is it, then?"

I had no idea how to explain it. "I've changed," I said. "And if our marriage is going to survive, then things with Craig have to change, too."

"But honey—" said my mother.

"I love him," I said. "But I don't know if I love him enough to *train* him."

"You make him sound like he's a puppy dog, Myrtle."

"Well he *is*, kind of."

"Yeah," my mother agreed. "A little bit."

As we talked, a bigger question crystallized for me—but I didn't say it aloud to my mother. Was I capable of returning home and holding my own, without falling right back into the ruts of our former relationship?

My father picked up the other line. "Girl," he grunted. "You all right?"

"Yes, Sir," I said.

"Then I'm gonna yank a knot in your ass the next time I see you," he said.

"No, you're *not*," I said. "I'm a grown woman, and I'll do what I please."

I'd never spoken to my father that way before. I'd never quite felt like a grown woman with him before. The line went quiet, and my mother whispered, "Well, Myrtle . . ."

"Well, nothing," I said. "I'm not a child, and I'm sick of being treated like one."

"You'll always be *my* child," my mom pouted, but my dad backed down.

"We took Craig out to supper," he said. "Told him to hang in there. All couples go through their hardships. You two will be okay."

I didn't say a word. I just stood against the far wall of the concourse and watched a golf cart full of old people practically run down a businessman who wouldn't step out of the way.

"Your daddy took Craig swimming with the manatees before he left," Mom said. "You know how he loves the manatees."

Craig's flaccid penis had always reminded me of a little manatee. One that got hit by a boat propeller. On the overhead speaker, an announcer made a boarding call. It wasn't for my flight, but I took that opportunity to get off the phone.

"Are you at the airport?" Dad said. "Where are you going now?"

Instead of answering, I told them I loved them and said goodbye.

I stood at the window, watched planes come and go, and dreaded the thought that in an hour, I'd be on one of them. I lamented the fact that my accidental pilgrimage had taken another turn. I wasn't ready to leave Vetiver or Raven Creek. In typical Myrtle fashion, I resisted in my heart.

There are spiritual teachers who say we shouldn't have preferences, that we should be open to whatever the universe sends our way. According to these teachers, if we don't have a preference, we don't suffer. But I see things differently. In my mind, there's plenty to be learned from resistance, especially if you've spent most of your life being a pushover.

MEATY TIDBITS

Sometimes quite unconsciously, we make happen what we want to happen, even if what we want is unthinkable. In hindsight, I realize that I must have needed an excuse to transform my relationship with Craig, and on the day that Vetiver passed out drunk in my truck bed, I'd finally had that reason. Up to that point, it was inconceivable that I could walk out of my marriage. Before my accidental pilgrimage, there was no hope for my relationship with Craig. But by shaking it up, by undoing our routines so completely, we created a possibility for something new, even if there was no telling yet what that something new would be.

People who have the means to travel to India and hang out with the Dalai Lama don't really have more of a right to enlightenment than you do. You don't have to go to Plum Village, the Omega Institute, or Raven Creek. For that matter, you can skip Sunday school. You just have to discover the lesson inside the life you're already living.

25

It was a boring afternoon, with nothing to do but wait and think. I purchased a souvenir hoodie in the gift shop, flipped through magazines and books, ate a pretzel with mustard, strolled up and down the concourse looking at travelers, and when there was only twenty minutes until my flight boarded, I went back to the pay phone, where I called Dottie.

"You know better than to call me during *The Ellen Show*," she said. "I'm too pissed off to talk to you anyway."

"You can watch the rerun," I told her. "I've got a lot to say."

But Dottie wouldn't let me start. "We've been best friends since third grade and you think you can just write me off?" she hissed. "Do you have any idea how that would feel? Did you totally forget how to empathize since you hit the road?"

"Whoa, Dottie," I said. "Hold on."

"A group e-mail, Myrtle? You just lump me right in with your mother-in-law and the Town Manager?"

"I'm sorry," I said. "I didn't have time."

"What's happened to you?" she asked.

"A whole lot," I said.

"I don't think you know the extent of your selfishness,

Myrtle. Did it ever cross your mind that people *need* you? You've always been the kind of person people can depend on. Now—I don't know *what* you are!"

"I'm not sure either," I said. "But Dottie, to be the kind of person that people can depend on is only a good thing *within limits*."

Dottie gasped.

"What I mean is—if your whole identity's wrapped up in being dependable, or if you're the person that *everybody* depends on, then you'll work yourself to death."

"I should've never asked you to drive me to my colonoscopy," Dottie pouted.

"I didn't mind driving you, crazy," I said. "It just got to a place where I was driving everybody everywhere, you know? I'm sorry it happened like this, Dot. I never wanted to hurt you."

"Humph," she said, but I knew things with Dottie were going to be okay.

I asked her then, "Have you seen Craig?"

"Seen him?" she said. "He's practically moved in with us—since he got back from Florida anyway. I guess you know he lost his crew?"

"Lost it?"

"He quit the water. Quit it completely. Roger heard at the Shore Stop that the boys on his rig had to take other jobs. They've got truck payments to make, you know?"

I hadn't pictured my leaving affecting him so much.

"Did you talk with him since he got the DUI?" Dottie asked.

"What?"

"Spent the night in jail, I hear. That was back Tuesday or Wednesday—after you called him from the rap concert and then hung up on him."

"It was a poetry reading," I said. "And he said the N word, knowing how I feel."

"Where *is* this Raven Creek place anyway? What state are you even in?"

"How do you know where I am? Where I *was*?"

"Craig told me. It showed up on his Caller ID. I wrote down the number and called you back there forty-leven-dozen times, but nobody answered." Her pitch kept escalating, and I could tell she was getting all riled up again. "Maybe you've got Caller ID yourself, huh, Myrtle? You screening your calls these days?"

"I'm about sick of your guilt trip," I said. "I told you I was sorry."

Dottie didn't reply to that, but I could picture her making snoot faces on the other end of the phone. Sometimes I wished we were kids again and I could just shove her in a mud puddle. It seemed like a good time to change the subject, so I asked, "How are my students doing?"

"Probably a lot better now that school's out for summer," she said. "I guess that with all you've had going on, you forgot the academic calendar." Then, with slightly less piss and vinegar, she added, "The last couple of weeks were a total wash. They ran off two substitutes *and* your classroom aid."

"I've missed you," I said.

"I missed you too," she admitted.

"Don't you have any *good* news?" I asked her.

"Just that you can probably get your job back—if you ever decide to come on home."

MEATY TIDBITS

If you're the kind of person that other people think they can count on, you might want to shake it up a little and start to wean your friends. By that, I don't mean you should become someone who can't be counted on—but rather you don't have to be the default. Take Dottie, for instance. While I was away, she went shopping with another teacher, a gal named Betsy Ann, and now on days when I can't join her at the movies or at Pampered Chef or Beauticontrol parties because I'm busy writing this devotional or preparing a talk for a lady's group, Dottie has Betsy Ann to fall back on.

Before you start in with that, "Poor Betsy Ann. Always #2" stuff, let me remind you that we're all Betsy Ann's to somebody. Don't lament this. Being second-runner-up, the backup plan, isn't such a bad place. Just make sure you don't end up being Betsy Ann to yourself.

26

When I saw my poor old banged-up, dusty, neglected truck after all that time, it made my heart happy. I never understood before why people name their cars and trucks, but now I do. A truck is more like a pet than a friend or family member. You never have to worry it'll be passive aggressive or mouthy. Even if the battery dies, it's not personal. You can't blame the truck for having a dead battery—especially if you've left the cell phone charger plugged into the lighter for almost two weeks, slowly sucking out the life.

Maybe most importantly, the truck doesn't blame *you*. It doesn't resist having those cold clamps from the jumper cables pinched onto its terminals, doesn't resist the sudden, harsh shock. It submits to the charging, cranks, and goes right on. Good old truck. Better than a husband that way. Probably even better than a wife.

"There you go," said the parking lot attendant who jumped me. He disconnected the cables and slammed down the hood.

"What do I owe you?"

"Nothing," he said, but I gave him a twenty for his time. In exchange, he tore up my parking ticket, winked, and wished me a safe trip.

I figured motel rooms would be cheaper outside the city, so I headed east, hoping to make it to the coast by dark. I still didn't have a plan, but I'd learned at Raven Creek how to ask for a dream before bedtime and be receptive to the messages provided by my unconscious mind. That's what I intended to do as soon as my head hit the pillow.

I was so tired by then that it probably wasn't a bad thing for my tire to blow out. It sounded like gunfire and woke me right up. I ducked—until I remembered I was driving and fought the steering wheel to hobble off the road. By then my heart had to be beating a hundred miles an hour. Luckily I was in a place where there was a shoulder for me to pull onto.

The back tire on the passenger side had a frayed gash blown clear through the rubber. Had I hit something? Maybe I'd been dreaming already, asleep at the wheel. Or maybe it was chance. I didn't know how to change a tire. I'd had a flat before, but Craig had fixed it.

But Craig wasn't there, and I wasn't about to call him. That left *me*. I found the owner's manual in the glove box (along with several hundred dollars I'd hidden from Vetiver), and I read the instructions. I shimmied beneath the truck enough to get the tire, soaking my clothes in the process. The underside of the truck smelled like earthworms and grease, and I nearly lost my arm when the spare finally dropped. But I wasn't crying or in the kind of panic you might expect. If I'd had a blow-out on a road only a month before, I'd have been a wailing mess. This time, I was just perplexed.

I couldn't get the nuts to loosen on the blown-out tire. I strained and pulled, strained and pushed, dabbing at the sweat running down my face with my shoulders as I worked. The nuts had been put on with a machine and tightened beyond my strength. They wouldn't budge.

"Damn," I said. Part of me was ready to beat dents into the truck with the tire iron, but I closed my eyes, took a deep breath, and slowly exhaled. When I opened my eyes again, I was staring at the ground and looking directly into a walnut shell—or half a walnut shell, to be precise—embedded in the dirt. It was like a tiny old face looking up at me, brown and wrinkled, with hollows for eyes and a beakish nose, and I thought, "It's Sister Esther," and then I thought, "No, it's *God*. The ancient face of God in that walnut," and then it asked me:

"What would a red fox do?"

I reached right over, pried up that walnut shell, and stuck it in my pocket (I've still got it in my jewelry box). I knew then that I had the option of simply spraying urine on the tire and bolting off into the woods. I wouldn't starve. The world wasn't going to end just because I'd had a blow-out.

I wondered if spraying urine might actually loosen the nuts. Then I remembered WD-40, more potent than urine in this situation, and I had an old rusted can with me behind the driver's seat. So I soaked those nuts. Then I positioned the wrench and jumped on it with both feet at once, using all my weight. The nut became a tiny mouse. I became a cunning fox. I pounced, and sure enough, the nut gave. All four of them gave.

It wasn't clear from the diagram where exactly to set up the jack, but I took my best guess. I cranked that jack around and around, and even though it was entirely mechanical, it seemed like magic to be able to lift up a truck like that. (I can understand why so many boys enjoy auto mechanics. It makes you feel like a superhero, lifting up a vehicle. More girls should give it a try.)

It wasn't easy, but I removed the old tire, rolled the heavy spare into its place, and positioned it. I wished Craig could see me. He'd never believe it. I tightened the nuts as much as I could with the intention of stopping at the next gas station to have the attendant check it. But I didn't stop. I kept right on cruising all the way to the Delaware coast.

MEATY TIDBITS:

Anytime you find yourself thinking, I wish _____ could see me now, take the time to examine that impulse. What is it you want that person to notice? Have you accomplished a skill? Stood up to a bully? What surprises you so much, and how would your world be different if someone else saw you as you now see yourself? Behind the immediate sense of accomplishment you'll find clues about larger aspects of your personality and relationships that bear examining.

The adrenalin that surges through your body whenever you encounter a sudden obstacle (like a dead battery or a blown-out tire) may keep you from thinking clearly for a while. If help arrives right away—in the form of roadside assistance or even a mechanically inclined parking attendant—then your anxiety will lift, but you'll be denied the chance to recover from the fright, think things through, and come up with a solution on your own. If help doesn't come, be glad-hearted! Trust that your own imagination will dilute the adrenalin. After that, you'll work it out yourself.

27

That night I stopped at a Super 8 on the highway, where the rooms were clean enough, though the sheets were thin. I didn't bother with dinner at all and never turned on the TV.

I dreamed I was sitting on a balcony at a different motel, one overlooking the ocean, and in the dream, the motel began burning down. I'd started the fire by accident and didn't even know it. I'd lit a candle, and the wind had come in through the balcony door and tipped the candle into my suitcase, which was full of costumes.

While the costumes burned and the room burned, I was writing a letter to Craig on motel stationery. What I had to tell him felt urgent. I had to write it down, once and for all, before it vanished the way a fin in the water disappears, UP and then under. I wrote, "Dear Craig: If dolphins swam in teacups, we'd never lose them."

But then the dolphin didn't want to swim in the teacup anymore. I looked into the cup, and the dolphin breached. It splashed water in my eyes, and while I wiped them, the dolphin leaped back to sea.

In the motel room, the carpet wiggled under flames, and fiery icing spread thick across the bed. But in the dream, I was watching the fire and also watching the woman, who was me, who didn't know about the fire. She was studying the ocean, marveling at how the ocean could crinkle and sizzle.

The woman who was me saw a sailboat in the clouds, and then the wind blew the sails away; just that fast, the sails were gone. I knew then that Craig was made of clouds, and I was made of clouds. I looked at all that water, at the way the foam on top looked a lot like clouds.

The fire alarm was going off, but I didn't recognize the sound. I heard the steady beeping but thought that somewhere below, a truck was backing up, and I wished it would stop because I needed to get back to my letter.

"Watch out," I wrote to Craig. "A person can disappear as quickly as bubbles after a wave."

The whole room was ablaze by then, but the woman who was me didn't know it. She was saying goodbye to the lavender horizon. By the time she'd noticed the sunset, the color was already fading. She'd been right there on the balcony, but she'd missed it. Then the sky turned the color of smoke and smothered the lavender out.

MEATY TIDBITS

Dreams are maps on the walls of your interior. Collect them, the way you might collect art. It doesn't matter if you understand them when you're awake. If you set the intention to collect them, you can go back when you're asleep, gaze again, and if necessary change directions.

If you're ever sipping from a teacup and find a dolphin there, drink quick. In the bottom of that cup, when the liquid is gone, you can see your primitive face, the face from before you were born, when you were still a fish yourself. Take what is untamed back inside.

28

I woke up feeling sick about that dream and wishing it'd had a different ending—maybe an image of me diving into the ocean and swimming off to a magical island. At Raven Creek, I'd learned that you can sometimes manipulate your dreams, wake up enough to take power and alter the outcome, and I wished I'd found a great big fire extinguisher on that balcony. (But would I really want to wear those old charred clothes again?) I wished I'd turned into a bird in my dream and flown away. Maybe everyone would think I'd burned up with my clothes, and then I could pass as a seagull for the rest of my life, dividing my time between the ocean and the Sonic parking lot scavenging for tater tots.

It seemed pretty clear that I shouldn't go home to Craig, though. Not unless I wanted to continue to live in a teacup, set fires I didn't see, and suffocate unaware. I stopped at a service station to have my tire worked on, and while I waited for the mechanic, I bought a muffin wrapped in plastic and a cup of coffee for breakfast. I was trying to be thrifty, knowing that my funds were limited, and knowing that sooner or later, Craig was going to raise cane about all I'd spent.

It didn't help that I had to buy a new tire, too.

Just inside the waiting room door, a bulletin board announced local events—a spaghetti supper, puppies for sale. It was covered with business cards and notices, and that's where I found the handwritten advertisement for waterside cabin rentals. I called the number, and when my new tire was installed, I drove out to see the owner.

It could've been a child's playhouse, this cabin, but it had a small refrigerator, a microwave oven, and a daybed. The bathroom was so little that you could sit on the toilet and wash your feet in the shower, if you ever had reason to do such a thing. The place was situated on a canal that led out to the bay.

"Seventy dollars a night," the owner said.

"For this?" I said. The wallpaper was bubbled and peeling, and the windowsill behind the daybed had started to rot.

"It's waterfront!" he said.

"Ditch-front," I countered, even though I liked the canal and thought it'd be fun to paddle around in if I had a canoe.

"You're killing me," he said. "Sixty a night. That's a deal!"

"Four nights for a hundred and fifty dollars," I said. (That'd get me to the weekend.) "Cash," I added. And he agreed. I couldn't believe it, but he agreed.

Maybe it was my newfound confidence that gave me the nerve to call up Craig, but my confidence took a nosedive when Miss Hattie answered the phone. She was cleaning our house. I could hear the dying down of the vacuum cleaner even as she said hello, and it aggravated me to think of her being there.

"Hey," I said, "It's Myrtle. Can I talk to Craig?" I felt like a teenager.

"You didn't hear?" his momma said, her voice breathy and dramatic. "He's in the hospital."

"What happened?"

"He drank too much whiskey and took some kind of pills. Terrible. They had to pump his stomach. I know he didn't do it on purpose, but the emergency room doctor called it a suicide attempt."

"Is he all right?"

"Well, no," she said. "He's a mess. He's *been* a mess."

"Is he gonna *be* all right?"

"Like you care," Miss Hattie said. "Why don't you do us all a favor and stay away from here?" She'd never liked me much. She'd always blamed me for not giving her grandchildren. "I hope he meets somebody in the hospital who loves him back," she hissed.

An image of Craig on a mental ward doing paint-by-numbers popped into my head, and I almost started crying. Then another part of me thought it might be nice for Craig to get to spend his summer painting by numbers, maybe on velvet. He'd never had a break from the water.

"Loving him was never the problem," I told her.

"Don't tell me you love him," she scolded. "Running off with that Negro. That's not the way you treat somebody you love."

"He's gonna get better then? If you're hoping he'll fall in love with somebody else?"

"He *better* get better," Miss Hattie said. "Or I'll wring his neck. I'd wring yours if I could reach it."

When I called the hospital, the nurse wouldn't let me talk to Craig. She wouldn't even say for certain if Craig was a patient and kept repeating phrases about confidentiality and the law. I didn't mention that I was his wife, and I didn't persist. But it upset me. Of course it upset me.

It also pissed me off. People leave one another every day, in a hundred ways, and the majority of those left behind survive it. Why did I have to be married to one who tried to kill himself? And why is it that leaving a marriage is more shameful than OD'ing anyway? If I'd stayed there, I might have OD'd too. Would that have made me more or less sympathetic?

I cooked macaroni in the microwave and chewed at my cuticles. I sat up on the daybed and cried onto my kneecaps. It had to be an accident. In all our years together, Craig had never done anything the least bit suicidal. He'd gone through some rough patches before—like everybody else. One time this fellow on his crew got hurt. They were out crabbing, and this boy got hot and jumped in the water to cool off. Craig didn't know it, and he turned the boat around and hit him with the propeller. It nearly cut off his foot, but the boy survived. He went on to become an accountant. He does our taxes every March and never charges us full price. After that, though,

Craig went through a period of heavy drinking, and once I found a little stash of pills I couldn't identify in a mint tin in his coat pocket. I flushed them down the commode and never mentioned it. But Craig got over it. He got better, like people do.

I wanted him to get better so I could leave him without feeling so bad about it.

MEATY TIDBITS

There are times when it's important to feel awful, when you should feel awful. Moreover, there will always be people who have the ability to make you feel terrible about yourself. In-laws can be particularly good at this, and we need these people, at least on occasion, to put us in our places. But feeling bad doesn't mean you have to change your behavior. You can feel bad and still maintain a steady course.

If you are a parent of a girl, make sure you teach her the importance of bargaining. So often women are taught to be pleasing and to not make a fuss that we accept things at face value, including sticker prices. Bargaining is a skill, and one that gives you power. You can bargain anywhere, even in a department store chain. Just ask for the manager and say, "There's a scratch here on this handbag. Can you take something off of the price?" If you're looking for a hotel, say something like, "For every two nights I stay, can you give me one night free?" You'd be surprised how often you'll get a break this way. When you walk into a restaurant, try something like, "We're here! We're your next party of three. Don't you have a free appetizer for the next party of three?"

29

The next day, I brewed coffee and took a cup outside to watch the morning crown. I sat out there by myself a long time, with just a pelican on a nearby piling. We had pelicans back home, of course. I'd seen pelicans all my life, but I'd never noticed before how their feathers resemble the skin on a coconut—or thatching on a roof, irregular and brown and kind of frayed and furry. I felt a lot like a pelican except I didn't know how to fly.

I wasn't sure what to do with myself. I couldn't remember a time when I'd had absolutely nothing to do, and I found it moderately terrifying. So I made a trip to the grocery store, picked up supplies, and drove over to the liquor store for some chardonnay. (In Virginia, we buy our wine in the grocery store, but in Delaware, they make you go the extra step.) I even went to the outlets and picked up a few summer things. When I got back to the cabin that afternoon, I lit up the barbecue grill and burned the old clothes I'd been wearing. They made a terrible smoky black stink, one that brought the cabin owner out to see what was going on.

It was scary to think of going home and scary to think of staying away. I called the hospital again where Craig was supposedly a patient and left a message. That evening it started raining. I'd found a fishing pole leaned up in the closet, and so

I sat on the daybed and fished right out the window. Nothing was biting—or maybe those canal catfish didn't like the hunks of cheese I was using for bait. I didn't care. It was nice to have my arms in the rain and still be sitting inside.

About nine o'clock, the phone rang. It was Craig. "I'm glad your cell phone's working again," he said. "I thought maybe you'd thrown it in the woods."

"No," I said.

"Why haven't you come to visit me?" he asked. "I thought you'd come visit, with me being in the hospital and all."

"I didn't know you could have visitors," I said. Craig exhaled, loudly, and didn't say anything else. I sat there with the phone in my hand watching a scene unfold across the canal. A pickup truck drove up beside a cabin a good bit bigger than mine. A man hopped out carrying a bag of groceries. He hurried to the door, fiddled with the lock until it turned, then flipped on an outside light. With the light on, I could see how hard the rain was coming down.

"My roommate's wife comes to see him every day," Craig said, sounding so pitiful it made me want to smack him.

"Good for him," I said, and we sat there in silence, both of us waiting for the other to speak. I was hoping he'd volunteer information about the suicide attempt. No such luck. Finally I decided to ask about it outright, but when I opened my mouth, what came out was, "Well, do you like him? Your roommate?" Like Craig had gone off to college or something.

"He's all right," Craig replied and let out another heavy sigh.

Across the water, the passenger-side truck door swung open and a woman stepped out. She was wearing one of those plastic rain bonnets that made her head look like a suppository, and I wondered why any woman would walk around wearing something like that. No man would ever wear such a thing. Didn't her husband see how silly she looked, and if so, why didn't he tell her?

"He's kind of different," Craig said. "My roommate. He's a Muslim." He said it with a "moo."

"Wow," I said.

"I didn't know we had any Muslims on the Eastern Shore, but we do. He's not the kind that sets off bombs or anything. His wife just wears regular clothes. Not one of those things over her head. They're not into that stuff."

The man across the canal ran back outside to retrieve a suitcase. The woman had peeled off her bonnet by then. She stood inside the entranceway, holding the door for the man as he splashed up the steps. It had been so long since Craig and I had been anywhere together. I couldn't even remember how long. It made me sad to think of how estranged we'd become. Now we were having this totally superficial conversation—

"Your momma told me you overdosed," I said. "What in the world?"

"The house was just so empty," he said. "It's been bad, you know? I swear, Myrtle. I thought we had a commitment and then for you to just leave like that. It's not fair."

"Maybe not," I said.

"You didn't tell me you were so unhappy," he complained. "If you were unhappy, you should've told me. You should've given me some notice, so I'd have a chance to change things before you just up and left me."

But how could he think I was happy? I had to answer to him for everything I did, had to get permission to drive after dark like a teenager. On top of that, I'd probably asked him to go to marriage counseling with me a hundred times. You don't invite somebody to marriage counseling when everything's hunky-dorie.

"I'm sorry," he said. "I'm just so confused. I mean—I didn't get it that you were so damned miserable." He kept shifting from sad, to angry, to sad again. "I know I can be an asshole sometimes," he continued. "I know I've been an asshole with you, and that's probably why you ran off and left me."

"Dottie told me you quit the water," I said. "Is that true?"

Craig cleared his throat. "I can't work," he said. He cleared his throat again, but this time his voice stayed grainy. "Not without you, baby. I can't even think straight." He was crying by then. "I can't eat. I can't sleep. I need you come on back now. This is tearing me all to pieces."

The only time I'd heard him cry before was when his daddy died. Maybe he realized we were dying, too. "Aww, Craig," I said. "Maybe you better stay there awhile. In the hospital."

"No," he said. "I need to be back home. With you."

The wind was blowing my way, and my face and hair and clothes were all getting wet. I reeled in my fishing line and pulled it back inside. "Hang on," I said, because I needed both hands to close the window. "Okay."

"Where you at?" Craig asked. "I'll come get you," he said. "Bring you back home where you belong."

"You don't get to decide where I belong," I told him.

"Yes, I do," he insisted. "You're my wife."

"But first, I'm my own person."

"Well, can't you be both?" Then the whine in his voice turned to spite. "When did you get so selfish?" he accused.

I can't tell you how much I hated being called that—selfish. If I'd been a dog wearing a choke collar and Craig had been a trainer with the leash, he couldn't have yanked any harder than he did. With that one word, he laid me right on the ground.

Craig sniffed and said, "Come on, Myrtle." His voice warbled when he spoke my name. "Can't we at least talk about it?"

I was sick of being the dog in our family. In my mind, I fastened that collar around Craig's neck. I picked up the leash, lashed it around my fist.

"Not until you change your ways," I snapped.

"I'll change them," he said. "Right now. I swear it. I'm sorry for everything I've ever done."

"That's your desperation talking," I said.

"Probably so," he agreed. "But I've been to group therapy

every single day since I got here. I know I've been controlling, but I'm gonna be a different man now. You wait and see."

Was it possible that he *might* be a different man? I'd certainly become a different woman. It was hard to know whether he was saying what he thought I wanted to hear or whether the idea of losing me might have nudged him along in his personal growth.

"Please, Myrtle," he said. "I thought you were a Christian."

"What's that got to do with anything?"

"Forgiveness and second chances and all."

"Oh, good Lord," I said. Before my accidental pilgrimage, hearing his emotions would have most certainly made me teary-eyed. Now that I've had time and space to process my own complicity in our out-of-whack relationship, it might make me cry again to hear him so desperate. But back then, when I was new to my power, his quavering tone made me act tougher than was necessary.

"If you can't say yes, then don't say no," he begged. He was so sorrowful. "It'll break my heart if you say no. You used to love me, didn't you? Can you just *not* say *no?*"

I wanted to strangle him. Didn't he realize that being such a low-down mopey Joe was a complete and total turn-off? Why would I want to go back home to that?

MEATY TIDBITS

Most women are afraid of being selfish. Sometimes men who know this use it to their advantage. But I'd rather be selfish than selfless any day. Before you can be good to anybody else, you have to be good to yourself. If you don't even have a self (as in selfless), how are you supposed to do that?

Sometimes we take pride in our failures, identifying with them and making sure everyone knows our flaws. Think of how Craig claimed he couldn't work because I'd left him. (For that matter, think back to how I told that dishwashing nun that God had spoken to me and I hadn't acted.) By claiming our failures, we excuse ourselves from having to do better and be our bigger selves. If we say, "I've always been scared of heights," then we never have to clean our gutters. If we say, "I have too much of a past to go into politics," then we cut off all thoughts of what good we might do if we were elected mayor. Look for places in your own life where you tout your weaknesses, and then consider if there's a payoff.

30

There was a state park not far from where I was staying, and the next day I decided to go there and clear my head. I borrowed a folding chair and a towel from the cabin, picked a mystery novel off the bookshelf, and headed out to the beach. I found a quiet place and sat there a long time, watching the tide recede. For some reason, there were rose petals in the sand. Maybe somebody'd just gotten married on that beach. I wondered about Vetiver and Flora, if they'd get married one day and if I'd be invited. I sat between rose petals and seaweed, footprints and tiny crabs. I took deep breaths and shallow ones, let in sad thoughts and happy ones. I swatted away no-see-ums and biting flies and buried my feet in the sand and kicked them free again.

Occasionally beachcombers passed. I watched flip-flops, bare feet, even sneakers cross between me and the water. And then I was joined by two children. They trudged over the dunes and dropped their towels not five feet away. The girl was maybe eight or nine and wore a purple one-piece swimsuit and too-big high-heeled shoes. The little boy was younger, pudgy, and tan. He wore red swim trunks, no shirt at all, and a yellow mortarboard on his head. Binoculars bounced from a string around his neck.

The girl turned to me and said, "He doesn't know how ridiculous he looks. Yesterday he graduated kindergarten."

"Oh," I said.

She let out a sigh, like this boy had exhausted her every day of his life, and then she marched along the shoreline like she was in a pageant, looking at shells, occasionally bending over to study them better. Her heels kept sinking in the sand. It was clear she'd break them soon, dragging them that way.

The little boy paced the beachfront, too. Sometimes he turned his binoculars up to the sky, and sometimes he crouched down, magnifying a snail or a crab. When the wind blew just right, I could hear him talking to himself or maybe to the sanderlings.

The girl picked up comb jellies from the edges of the surf, the clear small orbs that don't sting, and she stuffed them into her one piece, making breasts. I watched her adjust them, stacking one on top of the other, then digging down to retrieve the ones that slipped. She came back to her towel, spread it out, and then stretched there on her back, knees bent and high heels pointing toe-first toward the waves. She arranged her jelly breasts again, closed her eyes, and sunbathed.

It was funny how real she looked, playing pretend, but I knew she'd be stinking soon, with those jellies drying on her chest like that.

The little boy kept calling, "Roxie! Roxie!" but the girl ignored him.

"I found a nest," he declared.

"Who cares?" she called back without sitting up or even opening her eyes.

He looked again toward the trees behind the dunes. In a minute he started yelling, "There are eggs in it! Come see."

"Shut up, Ned," she said. "I mean it. You're being a nuisance."

The little boy threw out both arms, like he couldn't believe his sister would miss it. He looked at me, and I shrugged. "There are eggs in it!" he said.

Surely these children had been taught not to talk to strangers, but maybe I reminded him of his teacher. Maybe that made it okay, or maybe he was lonely. Like me. I stood up and met him near the dunes.

"It's huge," he told me, pointing at the nest. "See? Probably big enough for *you*."

"You think?"

"Maybe," he replied and giggled. "It might be a dinosaur nest."

"I'm pretty sure it's an eagles' nest," I told him. "Eagles build nests out of sticks and add onto them every year. Their nests keep getting bigger and bigger." I didn't mention that they sometimes crash.

He lifted his binoculars from around his neck, knocking off his graduation cap in the process. "Wanna look?" he asked. I helped him straighten his tassel before checking out what the eagles had done.

From that angle, I couldn't see any eggs. I could only see the nest itself, a side view. "Do you really see eggs in there?"

He laughed hard, like I'd asked the silliest question ever. He took the binoculars back, turned them up and cocked his head. "Two of them," he said. "Maybe three. Bluish-white—didn't you see them? We might get to watch them hatch if we come back tomorrow."

How could his vantage point be so different from mine?

I borrowed the binoculars a second time and backed up almost as far as the girl in heels to get a better perspective. I saw the thick green and rusty needles in the pine tree beyond the dunes, the tough scabby bark, the bend in the branch where the eagles had built the nest. I could even see scratches along the limb, but I didn't see any eggs. I was still searching when a voice said, "Please don't shade me."

"What?" I turned the binoculars on the girl, and it was the strangest sight, that skinny child with breasts moving up and down as she breathed.

"I want my tan to be even," she said matter-of-factly. "You're standing between me and the sun."

I apologized and moved my shadow away. The little boy had run out into the waves by then, so I left his binoculars with his sister. They were heavy and black, and the lenses were scratchy. When I was his age, I always confused which end of binoculars to look through. Maybe I still had it backwards.

That night, Craig called again. "Hey, baby," he said. "How you doing?"

"All right," I said. "How are you?"

"I suck," he said, and then he started laughing, this weird, hiccupping kind of laugh, like maybe he was trying to be chipper but really had his chin propped up on the barrel of a shotgun. "I thought it would be good to be home," he said. "But it's the loneliest place in the world."

Would he be manipulative enough to call me up, laugh in my ear, and then blow off his own head? "What are you up to?" I asked.

"Nothing really," he said. "I'm just out here on the deck watching the sun go down." He started singing the Elton John song about the sun going down, and I realized he was high. The sun had gone down a good while back. "I rolled myself a fat one," he admitted, "and now I'm watching the wind in that cottonwood tree."

Just my luck. I'd left him and he'd gone back to smoking marijuana. To my knowledge, he hadn't smoked in ten years at least. But maybe it was good for him to relax.

"Honey, I need a favor," he said. "I need you to come on home now." He just pestered me to death.

"I can't do that yet," I said, and I heard that word—yet— as it left my mouth, and I wondered where it came from and what it meant. Had I insinuated I'd come home later? "I can't," I repeated.

"You *could*," he replied.

"I don't want to," I said, more forcefully this time. "Craig, we're in each other's way. Can't you see that?" I thought about my afternoon on the beach. "We're throwing shadows on each other, standing between each other and the sun."

"But I *like* your shadow," he said. "Don't you like mine? You *used* to like my shadow."

I let out a whine. "You aren't listening to me. You never listen."

Just that fast, he kicked into snarl mode. "I'm listening, goddamnit," he replied. "All I do is listen, and all you do is blame. *You're* the one who changed," he said. "*You're* the one making all the decisions about *us*."

"About *me*," I replied.

"Go to hell, Myrtle," he said, and he hung up.

I poured myself a glass of wine and tried to relax. The wine was cheap, sweet, and disappointing. My head hurt. My eyes hurt. Part of me halfway wished Craig *would* kill himself. Then I felt even guiltier for thinking such a thing. I did some tai chi and took a shower. I was in my pajamas and already in bed when he called back.

He didn't apologize or even mention our earlier quarrel. Instead, he asked, "Remember that time I showed you how to make a bong out of a Pepsi can? And you singed your bangs trying to toke and hold the lighter at the same time?" He was calm again, probably high again, and I was relieved.

I remembered the smell, the crackling of my hair, like the crackling of the seeds when they lit.

"That was funny," he said. "You remember that, Myrtle?"

We'd been camping out in the West Virginia mountains. "That was a good trip," I admitted.

"We had a lot of fun together one time. We could have fun again," he said. "I'll get you a little Cadillac."

Like I'd ever wanted a Cadillac. Why would he think that I wanted a Cadillac?

"What are you doing?" he asked.

"I was just about asleep," I said.

We sat there a minute in the quiet. I could hear crickets, but wasn't sure if they were outside my door or outside his. Then

Craig threw in the offer that knocked the wind right out of me: "We could try to have that baby again," he said. "If you still want to."

I was forty-five years old, mind you. For years and years, when we were younger, I'd begged Craig to go get tested. There was something funny about his semen. It had gotten steadily thicker over time, but whenever I mentioned it, he denied it. He said his semen had always been that way and asked me how I knew what it was *supposed to* look like, implying that I'd seen semen that wasn't his. He had me crying in no time and swearing I hadn't been with another man. When I didn't conceive, he said it was because I wasn't committed to being a wife and a mother, trying as I was to grow a pecker of my own.

He'd been so awful. Why had I let him treat me that way and not left his sorry ass before?

Remembering it made my face burn. He'd made it all my fault. After a while, we had sex so infrequently that there was little chance we'd ever end up pregnant. I couldn't even imagine his body against mine anymore. Our marriage seemed as unreal as an eight-year-old with big old jellyfish boobies.

"It's too late," I said. "Damn, Craig. It's *too late*."

"Nah, baby," he said.

"You were so mean to me," I said.

"I wasn't mean to you all the time. I was nice some of the time."

There didn't seem to be any point in replying to that, so I didn't.

"Well, what you planning on doing?" Craig asked. "You gonna stay with Hellcat forever?"

"Vetiver," I said. "His name is Vetiver." I didn't even tell him that Vetiver was still at Raven Creek—or that at that very minute, I was only a couple of hours up the road from our house.

"That sounds like something a black woman would name a baby, don't it? Something you can't even pronounce."

"Goodbye, Craig," I said.

"Aww, hang on, sugar," he tried. "I didn't say 'nigger.' Why you getting all mad with me now? You gotta give me a break every once in a while."

"No, I don't," I said.

"Dang, Myrtle," he said. "You've lost your sense of humor."

"I reckon I have," I replied. "But I don't see what's so funny."

"You used to be different," he said. "Now you're a selfish old bitch."

And that was the end of *that* conversation because that's when *I* hung up. I didn't answer the next time he called, didn't reply to the voice mail he left apologizing and saying I was only a bitch a small percentage of the time. I had another glass of wine and told myself it was okay to be exactly where I was, but I didn't believe it. I kept thinking about those children, how the girl recognized that the boy looked silly, wearing his graduation hat on the beach, but couldn't apply that same discernment to her own stuffed swimsuit. Craig and I were in similar straits. It was the kind of night when I needed a visit from a wise red fox, but no fox came.

MEATY TIDBITS:

Most women have dreams of raising a family—I was no different—and here in America, we tend to think we're supposed to make all our dreams come true. In fact, if we don't turn our dreams into realities, we feel like we've failed. This is a problem. A big problem. Here's my take on it: It's fine and honorable to follow your dreams within reason, but you can't neglect to weigh the costs of those dreams. If I were to have a baby right now, it might come out with sixty-seven ears. As we grow older, some dreams need to be put aside. I'm not just talking about having children, either. Let's say you've always wanted to see the polar bears. That doesn't mean you should book a trip to Antarctica. Ask yourself: can I make do with seeing them on National Geographic? Would it be okay for me to not heat up the atmosphere to get there just so I can look at them in person? You don't need to fulfill every dream in order to live a fulfilling life.

Sometimes your shadow can get in the way of other people's sunshine. Be on the lookout for who and what your shadow crosses. Be sure to also pay attention to times when you're being shadowed by another person, institution, or belief system — and either ask that shadow to move or move yourself. We're all responsible for our shadows, but we're also responsible for getting our quota of good old Vitamin D.

31

On my last day by the canal, I went through all my receipts. The money situation broke down like this: when I'd left for my labia operation, I'd had just under three thousand dollars in my possession. Of that, I'd spent three hundred and fifty on motel rooms, a hundred and fifty on gas, two hundred and eighty on train tickets, nearly five hundred for the flight back to my truck, and several hundred more on food, clothes, a tire, and other sundries. But I still had fourteen hundred dollars from my surgery fund, and on top of that, I had another thousand I'd taken in cash advances off the credit card.

My plan was simple. I'd swing by home on my way to Flora's farm and repay the cash advance and interest. I'd gather up important documents like my social security card and bankbook, and I'd head south with the intention of figuring everything out before my savings was gone.

I needed to do something to mark the occasion, something that would always remind me, even if I returned to my same old life and same old ways, of who else I could be. So I looked in the phone book and found a tattoo studio not ten miles away.

Since Dottie and I had talked often about getting tattoos together, I called her up and invited her to join me: "Today's the day," I said. "My treat. It's the least I can do." A few hours later, we had a reunion just across the Maryland/Delaware line.

If we'd gotten tattooed closer to Raven Creek, we might have been able to find a Native American place where they played drum music, burned sage, and talked about the importance of pain to accompany new growth. But we had to settle for a regular old hole-in-the-wall place in a strip mall. Dottie looked suspicious. "Are we really gonna do this?" she asked.

"I am," I said.

She lit up a cigarette, and we leaned against the car and waited for her to work up her nerve while we watched customers coming and going out of an Asian grocery store at the other end of the block.

"I'm thinking about a starfish," she said. "Or maybe a seahorse."

"Did you mention it to Roger?" I asked.

"Please!" she said. "Not until it's irreversible."

The tattoo parlor was cleaner than I expected. There was hand sanitizer in the waiting room, and the artist, a fellow named Ribeye, wore rubber gloves just like a doctor and reassured us with his talk about autoclaves and fresh needles and ink. The walls were covered with thousands of designs: skulls and snakes, flaming motorcycles and eyeballs, cartoon characters, American flags, dragons and roses and smiley-faced moons. He had the music turned up too loud, and it switched between shrieks and bass lines that thumped in your temples. Finally Dottie said, "Can you turn off that noise? I can't even think."

"Seriously?" Ribeye asked and grinned. He probably wasn't twenty years old.

"Yes, honey," she said. "I've got some Stevie Nicks in the car. She's probably got some tattoos. You'll like her."

So we listened to Stevie Nicks while we flipped through the books. Ribeye showed us his album, a regular photo album filled with Polaroid shots, and he pointed out the ones he was proudest of—ones he'd free-handed rather than done from stencils or other people's designs.

I had serious doubts about letting him tattoo me, though. For starters, he was short, maybe not even five feet tall, and I knew he'd probably been picked on for it all his life, and that's probably why he rebelled and became a tattoo artist. I worried that his complex over his height might make him unnecessarily rough. He wore loose raggedy jeans and a sleeveless flannel shirt he'd left unbuttoned, probably so we could see the thick silver rings through both nipples.

"What are you looking for?" he asked me.

"I'm not sure," I said. "Nothing too big."

"That's cool," he said. "You see something you like, let me know."

I flipped through design books for a while and finally asked him if he had any pictures of foxes. If I had a red fox tattoo, I'd never forget to spray my urine.

He did, but the foxes all looked cartoonish.

"Images of scissors?" I asked, thinking of the body image workshop and Sister Esther's interpretation of how I needed to become more cutting. Ribeye had those too, but they looked like tattoos for barbers or tailors.

"I think I want a dolphin," Dottie declared.

"Dolphins are good," said Ribeye. "We got plenty of dolphins," and he gave her a book of nothing but sea creatures.

"The other night I had this dream about a dolphin swimming in a teacup," I offered. I could picture it as a really pretty tattoo.

"You are so weird," Dottie replied.

While I searched through the tattoo catalogue, Ribeye sketched out a curled up fox for me. Then he gave the fox glasses, and the glasses became the handles of scissors, and the scissor blades became part of the fox's ears. So I had both scissors and a fox in the same design. It was strange, but oddly fitting.

We went back to Ribeye's station, and he put that tattoo inside my right ankle. He warned me in advance that tattooing over bone wasn't the easiest, and even suggested that for my first tattoo, I get it somewhere meatier, on my back or breast. But I wanted to have the option of showing it off—or not—and I wanted to be able to see it myself.

The outline hurt the most. I turned my head away, and while the little zinger buzzed, we talked.

"How long you been tattooing?" I asked him.

"All my life," he said. (A funny answer, because he was still pimply and with dandelion fuzz for a beard.) "What do you do?" he asked.

"Teach school."

"What grade?"

"Elementary," I said. "Special Needs."

"Oh," he said. "Like the kids who wear helmets?"

"Mostly not," I told him. "Mostly ones who learn in different ways."

"I getcha," he said. "I got ADHD."

I couldn't think too long about that, not with him there working the needle. I wondered if he'd been in Special Ed, wondered if it mattered. (Would it be preferable to have an honors student as a tattoo artist? I knew some honors students who couldn't draw a sunshine if you started them out with a circle.)

He tattooed and wiped, tattooed and wiped. His needle hit deep, and I winced. Ribeye stopped his work, and I peeked down. He was just reloading his ink or something. "I've tattooed some schoolteachers before," he said. "But they didn't look like you."

"Oh?"

"They were more the party type."

Dottie came in then. She'd decided on her design, and she sat beside me on a stool and asked whether or not it hurt and commented endlessly on Ribeye's work: "Oh, it's bleeding a little. I can't look. Oh, it looks a lot better after you dab it off." The little tattoo machine whirred in time with Stevie Nicks on the CD player. I wondered if Ribeye had a girlfriend, and if so, what kinds of tattoos he'd designed for her.

And then my fox with scissors was done. She was a cute little fox, smart-looking in those glasses. Her eyes were flirty, but she could stab you with those steely sharp ears. He'd shaded her in such a way that she looked almost feathery. I liked it a lot and was sorry when he put a piece of plastic wrap over it. He cleaned up his station, changed his gloves, and then asked Dottie to lower her pants.

Dottie sat backwards in a chair, her underwear pulled low, and Ribeye tattooed the dolphin leaping right out of her crack. She moaned and groaned about it. It was a sensitive place where he was working, and at one point, I ran over to the Asian Market and got her some mango nectar so she wouldn't pass out. But in the end, her dolphin was a big success. Ribeye Saran-Wrapped her, too, and charged me two hundred and eighty dollars (I hadn't expected it to be quite that much), and we were on our way.

Dottie stayed with me that night, and after dinner, we sat on the daybed, drank chardonnay, and caught up. I learned that the principal at the elementary school hadn't honored my resignation. He'd chalked it up to a midlife crisis, and besides that, Dottie explained, it didn't make sense to go looking for another teacher so close to the end of term. Apparently my e-mail resignation wasn't valid anyway because it wasn't signed. Dottie said it could have been sent by anyone who'd hacked into my account.

"I don't even know how to feel about that," I said. "If I say I'm quitting, then I want to be treated like I'm quitting!"

"Are you sure?" she asked me. "'Cause isn't Craig Cribb on your health insurance? And didn't he just get out of the hospital?"

She had a point. There are spiritual teachers who claim that we're all just thoughts in the mind of God, but whether or not that's true, we still need health insurance.

"I guess I'll quit again," I said. "Officially."

"Well, fool, find another job first," Dottie suggested.

No sooner had we finished off the chardonnay than Dottie pulled another bottle of wine out of her overnight bag.

"Oh, Lord," I said. "We shouldn't."

"Pshaw," said Dottie. "Why not?"

It was the second time I'd gotten drunk in three weeks. Ordinarily I'm the sort of person who gets tipsy once every three or four years at somebody's wedding reception. I could beat myself up about it, but what good would that do?

So we drank and we talked, and we ate a whole bag of cheddar cheese popcorn. When enough time had gone by, we took off our plastic wrap and washed and admired our tattoos. The skin around Dottie's dolphin was all red and puffed up. She left her pants off so it could heal in the air.

I told her all about Vetiver and Flora, about Sister Esther and the others. I told her about the body image workshop and the story of the fox and the scissors that was my tattoo.

"Let me see it," she said. She was slurring a little by then.

"Again? You just saw it."

"I'm not talking about the tattoo," she said. "Let me see your dangler that got this whole thing started."

I got hot all over. Even my new tattoo got hot. But Dottie reveled in my discomfort. She cackled outright, rolled over on the daybed, and laughed into the pillow.

'It's not funny," I said.

"It is, too," she said. "Come on, Myrtle. You show me yours, I'll show you mine."

But I hadn't asked to see hers!

"I'll go first," she said. "Take a look." She yanked down her panties and spraddled her legs. "Well go ahead," she said. Dottie wasn't as modest as me. "I'm an old loosey-goosey," she said.

"But you hardly have any lips at all," I told her. Dottie's skin down there was darker than I expected, a little shinier, and she had an uneven scar running from hole 1 to hole 2 from her episiotomy.

"You wouldn't be so uptight if you'd ever had a child," she claimed. "Everybody sees everything you got when you have a baby. Lord, I shit right in the doctor's face, then had to see him every week at church. Your turn," she said.

So I did it. I pulled down my pajamas and let Dottie put the lamp right between my thighs. "Spread 'em," she said. "You're so bushy I can't see a thing."

I blushed, but Dottie didn't notice. She wasn't looking at my face.

"It's all folded over itself," Dottie said.

"I know."

"Well, pull it out so I can see," she instructed.

"No!"

"Just do it!" she insisted, and so I lifted the wing of my left labia and pulled it out.

"See," I said. "It's twice the size of the other one."

"Well, isn't that something?" she said. "You know what it reminds me of? Silly putty, when you pull it out like that."

"Ugh," I said, and let go.

"Springs right back into place, doesn't it?" she said. "I bet it's bigger on one side because Craig tugs on it."

"Not anymore he doesn't," I said.

"It's cute," she said. "It's like you got a little door to open."

"Shut up," I said.

"Knock, knock," she said.

I popped her on the shoulder and she popped me back. She turned off the lamp and I yanked my pants back up.

She poured us both another glass of wine. "You can stay at our house while you're working things out," Dottie said. "Kara's room's empty 'cause she's working at a summer camp. We got plenty of space."

"I can't face everybody, Dottie. Craig says the whole town thinks Vetiver's been poling my hole."

We both cracked up, and Dottie said, "So what?" She stumbled over to the refrigerator and found some graham crackers. I hadn't bought them. They'd been left by the renter before me, I guess, but I didn't mention that to Dottie. "Honey, I envy you, in a way," she said.

"What for?" I asked.

"Sometimes I wish I could run away, too, but I don't have the nerve."

It wasn't about nerve. Did she really think I had more nerve than she did?

"But my reputation," I said. "It's ruined."

"Shoot," she replied. "Once you've lost everybody's approval, you're finally free."

MEATY TIDBITS:

If you put your mind to it, you can learn to love the thing you hate most about yourself. You just have to change the way you think. Instead of saying, "my thighs are too lumpy," you can say, "my thighs have tiny moguls all over them." When you sit down on the toilet, instead of averting your eyes, you can let your fingertip be a skier and leap in and out of those little dimples. Pretty soon, you'll be feeling like your body is worthy of the Olympic games. You'll have turned yourself into a Greek goddess, just by changing your thoughts.

If you have a friend and you make her mad, don't assume the relationship is over (even if she says it is), and don't allow it to be over. Fight for your friend. Grovel if you need to. We all want to feel like we're worth fighting for. Buy her a gift. If your friend doesn't go for tattoos, take a class together, maybe pole dancing or the flying trapeze. Do something that contains an experience that you and your friend can share, and be sure that the experience you choose trumps the issue you've been fighting about.

32

The house didn't look like the kind of place where a depressed person had been hanging out. The windows were open and a breeze blew through. There were a few dirty dishes in the sink, but the counter was clean and wiped down. In the laundry room, the clothes had been washed, folded, and stacked up on top of the dryer, probably by Miss Hattie.

Purvis the cat was glad to see me, but not in any traumatized way. In the fridge, I found half a can of Fancy Feast and I fed it to her, just to get back in her good graces. Her water bowl was clean enough, her litter box far from tragic. I combed her to see if she had flea dirt, but she didn't.

In the bathroom, I discovered a damp towel on the floor, some toothpaste blobs in the sink, and the toilet seat left up, but all that was normal around our house. It didn't look like Craig's bathroom habits had changed that much since I'd been gone.

The mail was stacked up on the desk, and it took me a while to go through it. I checked our account balances on the computer and saw that my own paycheck had been direct-deposited, just like always. I paid the bills. Only one of them was overdue, and then only by a little bit. I realized I could walk right back into my life and nothing would be very different—except for me. Every day that I'd been gone, I'd felt like the world was spinning backward on its axis, so what did it mean, that I could return and things would only change a little?

What did it mean that if I *didn't* return, everything would keep right on going?

Craig's cousin was a teller at the bank. When I went to deposit the cash from the cash advance, I intended to get in the other teller's line, but apparently she wasn't working that day. Maybe she'd gone off on an accidental pilgrimage of her own. I had no choice but to wait for the cousin. My hands started sweating and smudged up the deposit slip, but the cousin said, "How you doing, Myrtle?" and punched in numbers on her special calculator.

"I got a tattoo," I said.

"You're brave then," she said. "I'd be scared to death." She handed me back the deposit slip, like it was any other day, and asked, "You reckon we're gonna get that rain they're calling for?"

It was surreal. Around town, even the bulbs on the north sides of the streets had popped up and bloomed. The boys outside the fire station were washing their trucks like usual. The old men in front of the convenience store smoked their cigars and waved as I passed. I wondered if I'd dreamed the whole thing up.

I drove out to the harbor, where Craig's truck was parked sideways on the clam shells. *The Lady Renee II* was right there in her slip, but Craig was nowhere to be found. So I went inside the Crab Cribb, figuring he must be helping his momma. Instead I found one of my old students, a sweet girl named Callie whose eyes darted around like tadpoles. She came out from behind the counter to give me a shy hug. "Hey, Miss Cribb," she said.

"You working here now?"

"Yes, Ma'am," she said. "Part time."

"Is Craig around?" I asked.

"No," she said. "He went out on the boat with Winston Stiles today. They should be back before long."

"Where's Miss Hattie?" I asked.

"Getting her hair fixed."

What had I expected? The world turned upside down? Even after all I'd been through, I was still situating myself at the center of the universe. To tell the truth, most times I still do—but I'm working on it.

I decided to leave Craig a note on his windshield, but changed my mind when I saw the mess the truck was in: trash everywhere, soda cans and Pringles tins, something sticky spilled all over the dashboard, the ashtray full of cigarette butts, and right there in the passenger seat, his release papers from the hospital all crumpled up. I guess Miss Hattie hadn't thought to clean his truck.

I wandered down to the dock and realized how much I'd missed it—the soft sloshes of the Chesapeake, smells of creosote and salt, calls of laughing gulls. *The Lady Renee II* looked abandoned and kind of naked out there without her crab pots. (They were all stacked up and tied down behind the Crab Cribb.) The boat wasn't in such good shape, either. Craig ordinarily kept it pretty decent, but there were fishing lines with hooks still on them rusting in the bottom. He'd left the plugs out so the boat could self-bail, but now there was half an inch of water all over, a brown skin of sludge in places. I had to be careful not to slip down as I mopped it up.

As nervous as I was about seeing Craig, it seemed important to do that before I took off again. Though I didn't have a lot of experience driving the boat and had never done it by myself, I decided to ride out and see if I could find him.

Some men (like Craig Cribb and his buddies) make women think that boating is more complicated than it is. I cranked off a couple of times backing out of the slip, but once I got it in forward, *The Lady Renee II* ran fine. And what a feeling—easing through the no-wake zone, the breeze on my cheeks. I passed some fellows coming in from a day of fishing, and they did a double-take, then waved.

Not enough men get to see women driving boats. We should give them more opportunities. I poked at the buttons on the depth finder until it started to work.

Having ridden along with Craig over the years, I knew exactly where the shoals were and how to steer clear of them. I knew how to find my way by following channel markers: red, right, return. So I boated out of the harbor and beyond the weir. When I'd run most of the water out and put the plugs back in, I threw down the anchor, just outside the channel, and waited for Winston Stiles and his crew.

After a while, they did. Naturally, they spotted *The Lady Renee II,* and they puttered over and cut the motor. Some of the fellows snickered into their shoulders, and Winston said, "See there, Craig. I told you it weren't no pirate got your boat."

"I'm half owner of this rig," I claimed.

"I see that," Winston said.

They sided up to *The Lady Renee II,* and Craig pulled the two vessels together. He'd lost some weight, mostly in his bottom. His pants hung loose and bagged a little around the top of his waterman boots where they were tucked in. His cheeks looked sad and droopy. He'd shaven recently, but missed some spots. "Permission to board?" he asked, in his best Coast Guard voice. I nodded, and Craig stepped in.

"All right," Winston said. "We'll see you back at the harbor, then," and off they went.

We talked all that afternoon and into the evening, and for the most part, our conversation was civil and sane, out there on the water. He tried to convince me to move back in that very day. I explained that I was heading down to SC to see my friend Flora.

"But you're coming back, right?"

"I don't know yet," I told him.

"You took a vow, Myrtle. You promised to be with me in

sickness and in health, forsaking all others, as long as we both shall live."

I saw him looking at my hands then. I wasn't wearing my wedding rings, and it choked me half to death to have him see me without my rings. I'd even debated putting them back on that morning—just to make it easier—but I knew by then that making things easier in the short term doesn't pay off in the long. "I did," I said. "And I meant it when I took it, too. But it might've been a lie."

That made him cry. It made me cry, too. We were quiet for a little while and watched the fish finder. Beneath the boat, all kinds of action was going down. We had rods and reels, but not a bit of bait.

Craig complained that I'd made unilateral decisions without him, and I agreed that it was true and unfair. But I explained that our unbalanced relationship had put me in the place where making unilateral decisions was the only way I could act. He was defensive sometimes, and so was I. But it was probably the most honest conversation we'd ever had.

Craig asked *me* to go to counseling with *him,* and I said maybe.

I asked him to change the name of his boat, and he said okay. Then I said, "You don't really have to do that," and he said, "Baby, if it means so much to you, I don't mind," and I said, "But everybody knows you by your boat's name," and he said, "People aren't stupid. They'll figure it out."

He said, "I'll buy you a little Cadillac," and I said, "Craig, I don't even like Cadillacs," and he said, "You're kidding," and I said, "No! Besides that, I want to pick out a car for myself," and he said, "Well, let's go car shopping, then." (But we didn't go car shopping until much later, and *The Lady Renee II* remains *The Lady Renee II* to this day.)

The sky turned pink-orange, and I said, "We ought to paint the boat that color," and Craig said, "That's going a little too far for me, Myrtle. I don't think I can do that."

MEATY TIDBITS

Sometimes the lies we tell don't show up for years. Lies like, "I'll be there if you need me," and "I'll love you forever." But if we didn't risk it and take a chance, we might never make a vow, and what a shame that would be, to live with such caution and fear. There's always a chance we'll have to break our vows, but we'll have a better chance of keeping them if we make the commitment in the first place. Before I left town, I actually signed my teaching contract for the upcoming school year, even though I wasn't a hundred percent sure I could keep it. But I told myself that if Craig and I ended up divorcing, it was important for our breakup to be amicable. For that to happen, we'd need to have contact. Even if I couldn't live in our house anymore, I could always rent a condo on the seaside. I told myself that if I needed a career change, I could push it into the future long enough to make peace with Craig Cribb first. One life change at a time still seems reasonable to me. Sometimes we need to make vows even when we're uncertain in order to create a picture of our future. That picture can guide us, even if the future doesn't manifest the way we expect.

A broken vow doesn't go away after you break it. Broken vows linger—sometimes forever. But if you try to keep a vow that needs to be broken, it starts to rot. It gets gangrene and oozes and weeps, and Lord, the smell. It's better to live with a broken vow than a rotten one.

33

When I went off to Flora's farm, I thought I had a lot left to figure out. As it turned out, I'd only be there a short while. You hardly ever know when your journey's going to be over—and when I say "journey," I mean it with a little "j" and a big "J," both.

I'd expected to help out on the farm, working in the strawberries or the soybeans or whatever Flora had planted. But she'd leased out her farmland, and except for a vegetable garden, she didn't have any work for me to do.

Still, she welcomed me, and Vetiver carried my big suitcase up to a guest room. "Relax," she told me. "Read. Rest. Put together a puzzle." But I felt like I was intruding, especially since it was clear that she and Vetiver were setting up a home together. So I took the dog and his tick and went for a walk around the property.

Flora's yard looked like something out of a children's storybook: big trees with Spanish moss draping down and roots wider than my thighs, grassy hills, daffodils poking up next to fence posts, squirrels everywhere, above us in the trees, and moths with speckled wings that disappeared into the bark as they closed. Ivy twined around a privet hedge; empty shells of cicadas clung to leaves and bark, even their eyeballs left behind, their claws.

I dropped down beneath an oak tree in the warm grass and tried to sort through all the things in my mind. In a while, Flora joined me there.

"You've picked one of the prettiest spots on these grounds," Flora said. She stretched out on her back, not worrying about whether there were any anthills beneath her, took a deep breath, and said, "Yes! It's good to be home."

"This place is gorgeous," I said.

"Everything here knows how much it's loved," she said. "Down to the last blade of grass!"

I thought she was speaking generally about loving the earth, but no. Flora's love was more intense than that. That's when she told me about communing with the over-lighting divas.

Let me see if I can explain this. According to Flora, a diva is like a plant's guardian angel, and the over-lighting diva is the big mama of all the plant angels in that particular region. There's a different diva for pine trees than for fig trees, for example. To confuse them is to diminish the value of each species, even though each is a part of the larger God essence. "You have to feel it to understand," she said. She put her hand on the oak tree, and I did too. Then Flora took my other hand and held it. "Relax," she told me. "Feel the energy."

The hard bark tingled a little against my palm and fingertips. My other hand, encased in Flora's, was sweating and tingling, too. Flora said, "Close your eyes and summon the over-lighting diva of the oak."

So I closed my eyes and did my best.

"Invite her to make herself manifest and be thanked for her work," said Flora.

It seemed like I could feel the bark shimmy beneath my hand.

"You see?" said Flora. "She hears you."

"Hey there, Pretty Oak Tree," I said aloud, and then I giggled, and Flora laughed too.

"You're doing it," she said. "It might seem silly, but you are." From Flora, I learned that you don't have to be a deeply spiritual person to call on the over-lighting divas. You can just be a regular old person with a garden. As you're out there staking your tomatoes and wondering why the little ones are rotting on the vines, as you're rustling through your zucchini and curious to understand why the green leaves suddenly have a milky coating, you can close your eyes, take a few deep breaths, and relax into the understanding that you're pure energy, and the plants are pure energy, too.

"Breathe deeply," Flora instructed. "And ask what the plant has to tell you. Your earthly bodies have taken different forms, but you're made from the same spiritual material."

Then she led me to another tree, hollowed out and dying.

"I guess it doesn't feel the love," I said.

Flora put both hands on the ancient truck and caressed it. "Love doesn't make you live forever," she replied. "And anyway, what could be more beautiful than a dying tree?" Chills shot right through me then, and I realized that Flora was a dying tree. Maybe I was a dying tree, too, and didn't even know it.

That night before I went to bed, I took a soak in the tub. It happened that the bathroom was next to Flora's bedroom, and I could hear her and Vetiver in there talking.

"Look how pretty your hair is," Vetiver said.

"My hair's not pretty," said Flora. "It looks like a possum. It'll look like a possum on the day that I die."

"What's wrong with that?" he answered, and then they were both laughing, so hard. It made me lonely and happy at once. I drained the tub and took myself to the guest room, and what I felt that night was bittersweet.

MEATY TIDBITS

The best gardeners and farmers know that plants must be thinned in order for others to thrive. There's nothing wrong with the plants that get pulled. There's no more or less God energy in the little cucumber you yank up by the stem and toss from the garden bed. You don't insult the little cucumber by selecting its sibling to survive and bear fruit, and ultimately you don't privilege the plant that gets to grow for the remainder of the season. The one that's yanked will return to the earth more quickly. The one that survives will succumb to weevils or frost. There's no need to have a preference or to assume that the cucumbers do. God is in them all.

If it seems at times that as individuals, we're powerless to create change, think about little beetles. Even the smallest beetles that live out their lives in shit and decay have the power to bring down majestic trees.

34

Flora's house had plenty of fans, but no air conditioning, so I slept with the window open, and I was comfortable enough beneath my sheet. It wasn't the heat that kept me up that night. It was the night-blooming cereus.

Next to the window, there was a cereus plant, maybe four feet high, and the leaves made soft rustlings with the breeze coming in, the ceiling fan on low. It sounded like the plant was whispering to me. I kept opening my eyes and seeing something moving in the plant. But when I'd sit up and look straight on, nothing was there.

Something else strange happened that night. It seemed like I could feel the sheet on my body in a way I'd never felt before. I had on an oversized T-shirt, and when I breathed, the fabric grazed against my nipples, and I could feel the sheet touching my legs, and not just my legs, but also my follicles. Then, too, there was the sensation that the cereus plant was beckoning to me. I felt soft and sleepy, but also electric.

I kept my eyes closed and my body still. But in my mind, I sensed my body moving over to that plant. The cereus's leaves became arms, waving me in. The plant embraced me, and I had an unavoidable urge—no a *need*—to put my tongue against the limber stalk. The moment I did, I was sucked entirely into that plant, pulled into the plant by the tip of my tongue.

Now I know how this sounds. Believe me I know—and

maybe I was dreaming, but I swear to you, it happened, whether it happened in a dream or not—and because it was the most intense experience of my life, I'm going to keep telling you about it even if you think I'm a whacked-out lunatic.

I passed into the plant, became fluid, pulsed through fiber and cell. All at once, I was in the leaf and in the stalk and in the root. I *was* that plant. There's never been a roller coaster to compare, because in addition to sensation, this union with the plant contained fragrance and flavor. Every cell of my body merged with that plant, and with all plants. I shot down through the roots out into the soil, and there was a universe in that soil— such activity—loam and rock and shell and manure, spore and insect and cilium. I thought, "This has been here all my life, and I didn't know." I thought, "It was there all along, back home in my hanging ivy over the sink."

Just that fast, I shot up through the roots of the ivy. I rose like fizz along those roots, exploded into the stalk and scattered onto the surfaces of leaves. I tickled those leaves; they shivered beneath me. They recognized me and laughed, and I laughed, and Purvis the cat overheard and came to see what was going on.

I dropped onto Purvis, effortlessly, like a sneeze, and I wandered through the wilderness of her coat, crossing haunches, exploring ears and paws. I circled her all over, traversed claws, nuzzled into warmth around her nipples. I was all over her at once, and she was purring, and as she leaped up the stairs, I rode her like a horse. She sprung high and landed on the bed beside Craig, who was asleep.

Then I was with Craig, and I could feel my body again, my follicles tingling, the sheet on my legs. Craig was naked and asleep on his belly, one arm wrapped around a pillow, and I lay there next to him and watched him breathe. I put my hands near his skin without touching, feeling the heat and energy rise and throb. I loved him with my hands, without ever touching his skin. Maybe I slept there with him, or maybe I slept at Flora's. It's hard to know.

I woke in Flora's guest bed to the sound of my phone ringing. It was Craig.

"I need to see you," he said. "I promise I won't stay long, but can I visit?"

So I said yes and gave him the address.

MEATY TIDBITS:

Some people don't allow themselves out-of-body adventures because they're too afraid of leaving their framework behind, worried that something could go wrong. They could get lost in the cosmos—or even lost in the plumbing. Others fear they'll return to find their bodies occupied by someone else, like a hermit crab that loses its shell and shrivels up (nowhere to go) and dies. I'm no expert on astral travel, but I can offer this bit of advice: Each time before I leave my body, I reassure it that I'm not vacating the premises for good. Then I bounce my spirit like I'm on a trampoline until I flip right through the top of my head. I look back at my shell, and send it love, creating a protective shield to swirl around my body and keep it safe. Then off I go! Sometimes I creep downstairs to be sure I blew out the candle on the stove. Sometimes I explore the house the way an ant might, climbing around inside the walls. Sometimes I visit with deer out in the field.

As surely as you're made from the same spiritual material as an oak tree, a night-blooming cereus, or a hanging basket of ivy, you're made from the same spiritual material as your husband, wife, or otherwise beloved. No matter how ugly things may get between you, don't forget that what you have in common is no less than the essence of God.

35

Vetiver woke up drunk. He came downstairs, made a pot of spaghetti for breakfast, ate it, and staggered back to bed. Flora didn't seem upset about it. She gathered her pocketbook and keys and asked if I wanted to ride to the meat market with her. We'd decided to grill out in honor of Craig's visit.

On the drive, I told her about my dream from the night before. Flora listened without interrupting, but when I asked, "What do you make of that?" she replied, "You seduced him!"

"I *couldn't* have," I said. "I was asleep in your guest room. Craig was back at home."

"You went wandering," Flora said, and I blushed. "There's no telling where you'll go next."

While the butcher prepared our order, Flora talked to me about sex. I tried to shush her, but it did no good. I worried the butcher would hear, but he was back in his little workroom running a saw. Flora said that she and Vetiver had an *exquisite* sexual connection, but attributed it in part to the work she'd done to keep her pelvic muscles strong. She asked me about elevator exercises and if I did them regularly.

"No," I said. "Not really."

"It's easy," Flora said. "Pull your vaginal muscles up one floor at a time, holding a few seconds at each floor. Try to go at least eight stories." So we stood there next to the lamb chops and tightened our pelvic muscles until the butcher came out. He showed Flora a steak. She wanted them thicker and with less fat. So away he went.

"You have to ride your elevator back down, too," Flora said. "Go up and down, up and down."

She told me it'd been a long time since she'd been in a relationship, but she'd done lots of solo practice to stay in shape. Then she raised her bushy gray eyebrows to be sure I understood.

Well, naturally, that made me squirm. I wandered over to the chickens and pretended to look at the prices on boneless thighs.

"Please tell me you have a good sex life with your*self*, " she said.

I shook my head. I wasn't a prude or anything, but I hadn't felt sexual in so long. I'd gotten so accustomed to resisting Craig's advances that I guess I'd shut down completely. Now it seemed like I might be waking back up.

"You have a vibrator, don't you?" Flora asked

"Flora!" I said, and I cut my eyes over to where the butcher in his little room was wrapping our steaks in paper.

"Well, you need one," she said. "Everybody does! Sometimes you can't please other people, but you can usually please yourself." She picked up a couple of onions and some baking potatoes from a bin in the middle of the store and sat them next to the cash register. "They sell 'em at the drugstore. We'll get you one on the way home."

So Flora bought the steaks, and I bought the Colt 45, the Budweiser (I wasn't sure Craig liked malt liquor), and the vibrator. Thank goodness they didn't look like the kind you'd get at a dirty bookstore. They sold them right there with the hair dryers—personal massagers, they were called. I didn't open the package for nearly another month, but since that time, I've come to appreciate the wonders of personal massage.

At the end of the driveway, Flora stopped the car, and I jumped out to get the mail. Along with fliers and bills, I found two different packets of information about alcohol treatment facilities.

"He's going to rehab?" I asked.

"When he's ready," she said. "We're educating ourselves right now. Finding out what's available."

I liked it that Flora didn't treat Vetiver's alcoholism with too much drama. It was part of the larger package. Not a great shame or emergency and certainly not a deal-breaker.

That afternoon, Flora used the Weed Eater to clean up around the deck, and Vetiver danced behind her with the broom, dusting off the boards and bricks. I watched them from the kitchen, where I washed potatoes and rolled them up in aluminum foil for baking. They didn't resist one another. They didn't try to change one another. Maybe that was their secret.

On the other hand, they'd been together less than a month. I'd logged twenty-three years with Craig Cribb, so it was no wonder we didn't dance around with Weed Eaters and brooms.

When Craig arrived, Vetiver moseyed out to the front yard to greet him. Craig shook his hand, but I wasn't sure what that meant. Just the year before at SchoonerFest, I'd witnessed Craig shaking hands with a candidate for House of Representatives, a man he considered a crook and a scoundrel. So shaking hands with Vetiver could mean anything.

"Your daddy was a fine man," Vetiver said.

"He sure was," Craig agreed.

Then Flora took Craig by the arm and offered to show him around the homestead. It was awkward, of course, but Flora made it better. She led Craig through the barn and the springhouse, telling him the history and legends of the land, while Vetiver and I followed behind, occasionally shrugging and glancing at one another. Then we all sat out back on the deck, and the fellows had a couple of brews while Flora cooked the steaks. (You'll be glad to know I stayed completely sober that night. My rationale: if Craig picked a fight with Vetiver, I wanted to be able to drive to the hospital.)

To avoid the flies and mosquitoes, we ate our supper on the screened-in back porch. There was just enough light to determine which of the steaks were medium and which were rare. We sat around a picnic table, me and Craig on the side facing the yard, Flora and Vetiver on the side facing the kitchen, the dog and his tick on the concrete floor beside us, and we feasted. Except for a single candle in the middle of the table and for the light inside the kitchen behind us, we were in the dark. I was glad. It made it easier to talk. Everything's so much softer in candlelight.

"So, Vertiver," Craig said. "What you planning on doing with yourself next?"

"It's Vetiver," I corrected. "There's no R in it."

"That's what I said," Craig replied. "Vertiver."

"Just call me Hellcat," Vetiver said. "Old habits are hard to break." He winked at me and continued, "We got some maintenance to do around this place. We're gonna refinish the floors, for one thing."

"That's a big job," Craig said.

"You know it," Vetiver replied, and then they talked about sanding and different kinds of finishes, linseed oil and beeswax, and I relaxed some. Craig's the kind of man who appreciates hard work and tends to respect do-it-yourselfers.

The conversation shifted to the fishing industry and the regulations on blue crabs. Craig told us he was putting together a new crew. "I got a fellow lined up for next week," he said. "But he's temporary." He looked at Vetiver and added, "If you want some work, let me know. I'm looking for a few good men."

Well, it shocked the tar out of me for Craig to make that offer. I couldn't tell you what I did with my face, but Craig must have thought I was about to jump him for being sexist because he turned directly to Flora and said, "It's hard work. You have to haul up these heavy crab pots and all, but I wouldn't be opposed to having a woman on my crew, if you wanted to give it a try."

Really, it was too much. I couldn't tell if Craig had actually changed or if he just wanted me back.

Flora smiled at him, like she might be considering a new career as a water-woman.

"I appreciate the offer," Vetiver said. "But I think I'm gonna stay around here," and Craig nodded.

We cleared the table, and I started a pot of coffee. Flora brought out the pie, and we kept on eating. Vetiver had a cooler right there on the porch, and he helped himself to another can and offered one to Craig. We listened to the crickets chirping, and in a little while Vetiver said, "I got a drinking problem, as you know." He held up his Colt 45, gave me a sad, sideways smile. "I know I need to work on it. I've been *wanting* to work on it, but just didn't have a good enough reason." He reached out and took Flora's hand. "Now I do."

Flora reached across with her other hand and patted his arm. "You don't decide to get sober any more than you decide to start walking on your hands," she said.

"Might be easier to start walking on your hands," Vetiver replied, and we all laughed. "I'll probably have to go off somewhere to get some help. We're looking into some places."

"That's what you ought to do," Craig said. "Takes a big man to know when he needs to ask for help." Flora's dog wandered over and flopped beside Craig. He reached down and scratched the dog behind his ears. "It's not easy—asking for help, I mean. That's what I'm doing here, you know? I'm trying to ask for help, too. Cause I want my bride back."

He said that. My bride. And oh, I could've died. I could've killed him, but he was doing the best he knew.

"That's the spirit," Vetiver said.

About that time, Craig discovered the tick on the dog's ear. Without a second thought, he dug his fingernails around it, plucked the tick off, and popped it bloody between his thumb and forefinger. You could hear it, a tiny little burst. "I'll do whatever it takes to get her back," Craig said. He wiped off his fingers on his pants leg and continued stroking the dog.

Talk about awkward. But oddly enough, Flora or Vetiver didn't either one seem to care. Nobody mentioned it. The dog didn't cry out or even move. Nothing happened at all—except that Craig kept right on talking. "I'll never forget the day I fell in love with Myrtle," he continued. "The day I *knew* I was in love.

"We'd gone to the movies up the road," Craig said. "And while we were there, it came a big rain. Poured down rain. But by the time we drove back into town, it was just drizzling. We come up along Washington Street, and all of a sudden there was this pop, pop, pop, pop. I slowed down, and it was good and dark, and with the rain and the windshield wipers, we couldn't tell at first that the road was full of frogs."

"Frogs!" Vetiver said.

There had been so many frogs. Frogs everywhere.

"I hit the high beams and saw them jumping around. You couldn't move without running over a frog. Then Myrtle made me stop the truck, and she got out and started lifting the frogs from in front of the wheels."

He laughed. "You should've seen her! First she tried to shoo 'em, but you know a frog don't give a damn about being shooed. Then she kicked at 'em with her feet, but soon as one would hop out of the way, another one would take its place.

"I said to her, 'Get on back in the truck,' 'cause it couldn't have been more pointless. I'm telling you, there must've been a million. But Myrtle kept right on moving 'em. She was drenched, too. You could've wrung her like a dishrag. She'd say, 'All right, drive up a little bit more—whoa!' and then she'd move another one outta the road."

"I'm not surprised," Flora said. "Myrtle has a tender and generous heart." (And it touched me for Flora to say that, considering the episode with the tick. Maybe I was looking even *more* generous now that Craig had gone and killed it.)

"Did you make it all the way home?" Vetiver asked.

"Shit!" Craig said. "We didn't make it twenty yards. After a while, she cleared the way for me to pull over, and we left the truck parked there 'til morning. I walked her home. Weren't but four or five blocks to her house. You remember that, Myrtle? We had to tiptoe all the way!"

"Of course I remember," I said. Craig had laughed and laughed about it. He'd told all his friends. It seemed impossible that he could have fallen in love with me then. "But you've made fun of me for that all my life."

"Well, yeah," Craig said. "What'd you expect? Picking up frogs in the road!" He laughed and punched my shoulder lightly, like we were the oldest and dearest of buddies.

Not long after, Flora moved over to a rocking chair. She was clearly getting tired. Vetiver visited with us a little while more, but I started yawning, and it was Craig who finally said, "I reckon we'd better call it a night."

Craig stood up, woke Flora to hug her goodbye, and shook Vetiver's hand. "Thank you," he said. "I sure enjoyed it."

"Aren't you staying?" Flora asked. "There's a pull-out couch."

"Nope. I made a deal with Myrtle that it'd be a short visit, so I'll be hitting the road here directly."

He stayed long enough to help me close up the grill and pick up the empty beer cans. "You okay to drive?" I asked.

"Not going far," he said. "I got a room at that little Travelodge right there at the highway." He pulled a key out of his pocket and dangled it. "You're welcome to come with me," he said. "I'll bring you back in the morning."

I smiled and shook my head. "I'll walk you to your truck," I offered, and so we strolled around to the front yard where he'd parked. But we stopped beneath that dying, hollow tree and Craig put his arms around me and pushed me against the bark.

"Remember when we used to go hiking up on Skyline Drive?" he said. "This reminds me a little bit of that."

"It's been a long time," I said.

He rested his chin on top of my head. "Feels like yesterday," he said. It felt pretty good to have him close, with the tree at my back, and I nuzzled a little against his neck.

"We were just children," I said. "Practically." He'd bent me over every rock in the Shenandoah River. I wondered if my labia had been big back then, too. I wasn't sure if it'd grown over the years or if it'd always been that way and just took me a long time to notice.

"I know I've been hard on you sometimes, Myrtle. I know I can be a shit. But I intend to change that," he said. "I really do." His hands were under my shirt, slipping up and down my back, then underneath my bra. "I missed you," he said.

I *knew* what he missed.

He was undressing me by then, and I wasn't stopping him. I didn't want him to stop, not really. It'd been so long since we'd made love—and years since we'd made love in the great outdoors. Maybe there was a time when we'd have done it standing up, but I'd gained too much weight, and he had weak knees. We dropped right down in the rough grass that Flora loved so much.

He tugged at my plus-sized labia and pushed it out of his way. "I love you," he said. "Every bit of you."

"Not *that* bit," I said.

"Don't close me out," he said as he pushed in, and it was more than a little bit complicated, in the moonlight, the root of a dying tree against my cheek, extraordinary and so confusing at the exact same time.

MEATY TIDBITS

When you're feeling at-odds with someone you were once close to, it's important to clarify what the problem between you is. Sometimes we get caught in a circle of hurting one another without fully understanding the reasons. I'll give you an example that Flora gave to me. Flora has a gay sister (named Fauna, of all things), and apparently, Fauna got her feelings hurt because Flora never visited. She felt so rejected that she stopped visiting Flora in return. Soon they only talked on the phone on holidays. "She thought I didn't visit because she was gay," Flora said. "When actually it was because she had three long-haired cats. Back then, I had allergies."

Sometimes when you're feeling ambivalent, and you can't decide what's right or wrong, sometimes when it seems like what's best might be what's worst (like when you're trying to decide whether or not to have sex with your estranged husband, wife, or otherwise beloved), you have to simply make a decision. Even without certainty, you can leap to one side or the other. Follow your hip bones deliberately in the direction that you land.

EPILOGUE

I returned to the Eastern Shore of Virginia only a few days later, but I didn't move back home. Dottie's husband's mother had recently gone into assisted living, and they hadn't made up their minds yet about what to do with her house. So they offered it to me, rent free as long as I cover the utilities and keep the grasses trimmed. It's a little cottage at the end of a remote farm lane, no more than eight hundred square feet, and it's been the perfect place for me to get my bearings.

Craig resisted the move, even going so far as to forbid it (he'll have to work on *that* little habit if he ever hopes to win me back), and he swore he wouldn't help me with my boxes. But in the end, he loaded my things into his pickup and hauled them out to the country. I invited him to stay around while I unpacked, and he cooked us some crab cakes for supper and only pouted a little. There was one condition to our separation. I promised to go out with him at least once each week. So we're dating now, and so far, it hasn't been a total disaster. In addition to getting together to watch movies, he's taken me to a horse show, a monster truck rally, and to the Barrier Island Museum. I've taken him to the theatre, to a barrel tasting at a local winery, and to a weekend Healing Touch workshop. We haven't made a big deal out of our separation, and so it hasn't been a very big deal for anybody else. Even old Miss Hattie tolerates my company when she has to.

For so long, I thought Craig Cribb was the one who needed

to change, but my life didn't actually get better until *I* did. Who knows what'll become of Craig and me? It's really too soon to say. On more than one occasion Craig and I have commiserated over how hard marriage once seemed—when actually, the only thing you have to do to stay married is not file for divorce. Some nights Craig sleeps over here, and some nights I sleep over there. But nine times out of ten, we sleep alone. Some days I spray my urine, and some days Craig sprays his. I think it's true for both of us that marriage feels more manageable now that we imagine it in smaller chunks.

Right after I left Flora's farm, Vetiver admitted himself to an in-patient treatment facility. He stayed for six weeks and then moved back in with Flora. But only a month or two later, he called me from a bar, slurring and crying into the phone. I couldn't understand a word he said, and couldn't get an answer on the phone at Flora's house. I thought for sure she was dead and drove the four hours down there planning her funeral. But she was out back in her chicken coop, mending the brooder. Vetiver'd passed out drunk under the oak tree by then, and Flora'd left him there, covered up with a wool blanket. I helped her drag him inside, and as soon as a bed came free at Grace Place, we checked him into rehab again.

The two of them came here for a few days at Christmas. They stayed in our house, in the guest room, and we all cooked together. Craig grumbled about it when I insisted he put his homemade holiday wine behind the seat of his truck so Vetiver wouldn't be tempted, but he got along fine and just kept running outside to have a sip every now and then while the rest of us sang carols. We opened presents together, played board games and cards, and even took them to the Christmas party at the hardware store, where nobody around town could believe Vetiver was the same man they once knew as Hellcat. "Oh, yeah," he said. "I've come up in the world now that I've got a good woman by my side." He meant Flora, of course, but I like to think that I was the good woman that got him started.

In the winter, Vetiver even reconnected with his daughter and met his grandchildren for the first time. He told me on the telephone how he and Flora'd gone to Charleston to see a specialist about her cancer—not an oncologist, mind you, but a practitioner of black-grape therapy who claimed you could cure cancer entirely by eating nothing but dark grapes. After they'd finished at the grape clinic, they met up with his daughter and her family at the Battery, where they walked through the park and even rode around town in a horse-drawn carriage. They'd made plans to get together again over the summer.

But in April, he was cleaning out the garden shed and accidentally upset a wasps' nest. The doctors never said how many times he was stung. By the time Flora found him, he was blue and couldn't breathe. He didn't even make it to the hospital.

"Was he allergic?" I asked Flora.

"Evidently," she said. "He never once mentioned it. I had no idea. I wonder if he even knew."

After reading up on wasp stings, it seems even more bizarre that Vetiver would die that way. You almost never get stung in the springtime. Wasps sting in autumn, when they're pissed off about being so hot and crowded by all the others in the nest. From all we can figure, he must have made direct contact, grabbing onto that nest somehow. I picture him reaching for something on a shelf, a can of WD-40 or replacement string for the Weed Eater, and wrapping his hand around something he hadn't intended.

Craig and I drove down to be with Flora. Her eyelids were bloated from crying, and she kept a handkerchief stuffed down the front of her blouse, another one tucked up her shirtsleeve. She was skinny from all the black grapes, or maybe from the cancer, and Craig turned out to be better at comforting her than I was.

I was too mad to be a good friend. I can only hope that in some way, Flora took comfort in my anger, knowing I loved him, too, knowing I didn't want to lose him either. I kept crying about how unfair it all was, silly as that sounds. Part of me wanted to make killing wasps my life work, but Flora reminded me of the irony of it all—how a fellow like Vetiver Faulk, who you'd expect to die from a compromised liver or maybe a drunk-driving crash, could cross to the afterlife so innocently, so unexpectedly.

"I hope I get to go that way," she said. "Just going along about your business, having a perfectly ordinary day and then bumping headfirst into death." She honked her nose and offered Craig some cake.

"I keep picturing it like reading a book," Flora said. "You're reading along, enjoying the story, or maybe even bored with the story, and suddenly you see that you're at the end, when you thought you still had chapters to go. You didn't even know it, and the story's over. There's nothing else left."

"Huh," said Craig.

"It must be like that, don't you think?" Flora said. "Such a surprise when death finally shows up."

I left them at the table. I went outside and stomped all over that property. And I cried. Lord knows I cried. I stood there at the garden shed door, my head on the corrugated metal, and I beat it with my fists like that would do any good at all. Flora said to me, "Call on the over-lighting diva of the wasps and talk it out."

"I don't want to talk to any old damned wasp," I argued, and I wiped my nose on my sleeve.

"Wasps do good for the world, Myrtle," she told me. "They keep us from needing pesticides by eating the parasites that'd otherwise kill off the vegetables."

"They stung him to death," I said. "I don't give a damn what good they do for the world!"

But that was just an outburst, caused by my grief. I do give a damn. I do.

Too often we think of life and death as entirely separate things, when they aren't separate at all. You die to one way as you're born to another. If this seems terrifying (and it does to me), if you find yourself scared of changes, large or small, look to the clouds for guidance. The clouds don't question or resist. They blend and separate without care. I couldn't do much about my grief over Vetiver's death, but I could acknowledge the clouds. I could try to behave more like a cloud.

There was a time when I thought that my accidental pilgrimage would provide me with answers to life's big questions, but the questions never end. As soon as one gets answered, another one shows up: How will we get through this season of sorrow? How do we change the tire on this truck? What happens to trust once it's been lost? What if the train can't get me back home?

What will we do about all these addictions? What might fly out of that hole in the ground? How will we save this thing we call marriage? Where will we go when the motel burns down? The mundane, the sublime, they all get mixed together. You could go on a pilgrimage every day of your life and still not understand it all.

This summer I'm headed back to Raven Creek for a week, where I'll be sharing a cabin with Flora, her dog, and any ticks or tumors, foxes or wasps, Locklears or children with binoculars that happen to join us. I'm imagining it as a cross between summer camp and a family reunion, because spiritual breakthroughs are every bit as apt to happen at the beauty parlor or the bus stop. (But who'd want to spend a week *there*?) So I leave you now with the hope that this little book helps you open yourself to your own journey—and not just to the joys but also to the miseries. When uncertainty or suffering arrive in your life, recognize them as old friends and teachers. Greet them with a hug. Say, "Thanks for stopping by." That's all there is to awakening, really. It's not especially easy, but it's not especially hard.

APPENDIX

When my old friend Jenean, the Special Education Director, heard about my adventures, she suggested that I come up with some exercises for the new teacher orientation. Things went so well that I was soon asked to do one for the returning teachers. Then the Literacy Council had me run a program for their Annual Directors Retreat. In this way, a new vocation was born. I'm including here some of the exercises I've used in case you'd like to try them at your own events. Feel free to modify them for your purposes.

Read aloud the following passages and questions, and allow fifteen minutes for private reflection and journaling. Then come together to share.

ON SUFFERING AND NONRESISTANCE

Once upon a time, there was a day trader who invested badly and lost everything he had. He wound up hiding out in the mountains, eating berries, and sleeping in caves. At his lowest point, he had whole colonies of lice camping in his armpits. As you'd expect, it turned him wild and frenzied. He clawed himself bloody, until at some point, he stopped scratching.

In spite of how he itched, he just stopped scratching. Lo and behold, the terrible itching left him. Nowadays, you can listen to him in your car, on your way to and from work, and his serene voice will assure you that nonresistance is the solution to every problem, from fleas to infidelity to fear of death.

1. What kinds of personal itches must you endure? Has your beloved child left for college? Do you share an office with a coworker who listens all day to talk radio? Try to identify at least three different types of itches in your life.

2. What form does your scratching take?

3. Are there any payoffs to scratching? In what ways does it help?

4. What would it look like if you stopped scratching? For today, how might you incorporate nonresistance into your life?

ON LIES AND TELLING THE TRUTH

Most any fifth grader can tell you the story of George Washington and the cherry tree, how when his father confronted him, he replied, "Father, I cannot tell a lie; I chopped down the cherry tree." Even today, we celebrate George for his honesty, not questioning why he confessed or taking into account the outcomes of that confession.

Imagine for a moment that the tree had been planted and tended by a doting grandparent who was about to pass on to eternity. After Little George admitted that he was the one who walloped it with the axe (and not some poor Native American with smallpox who needed the firewood), his grandpa spent his dying hours looking out the window at the stump, disillusioned about his beloved grandson who'd already forgotten his mistake and was off playing conqueror in the woods somewhere. Wouldn't it have been better for George to wait until after his grandpa's funeral to tell the truth?

Sometimes when we blurt out the truth, we do it to alleviate our own pain and not for the good of other people at all. A lie or wrong action produces a certain amount of misery; confessing relieves the pressure. To all you liars and would-be liars out there, before you confess, ask yourself: "Who am I doing this for?" If you're doing it to relieve your own great misery (even if there will be some smaller misery in the confession and its aftermath), hold it for a little while, until you're sure the timing is right.

1. Make a list of lies you've told, large and small.

2. Which lies did you confess? Did it help? How?

3. Which lies are you still keeping? Have your feelings about the lies changed over time?

4. When have you told the truth in an effort to alleviate your own pain?

5. Are there times when you would rather be lied to than told the truth? Why or why not? What would you rather not know?

6. Is it possible to make amends for a lie without telling the truth? How?

A similar set of questions may be asked about the keeping and breaking of vows. Here are a few to get you started.

1. What vows have you taken? Why did you initially take these vows?

2. What vows have you broken? If you could make your broken vows disappear for good, would you banish them from your memory? Why or why not?

3. How do vows you made thirty years ago look today? Has the texture, smell, or color of your vow changed over the years? Does the vow fit you better or worse than it did when you first took it?

If time allows, have participants make collages to represent the vows they've taken and the vows they've broken. Provide magazines, scissors, markers, and poster-board for this activity. Be sure to remind participants to take into account the evolution of their vows.

ON FAILURE AND SUCCESS

Sometimes we create misery for ourselves by using the wrong measuring stick to gauge our progress. When you measure success across different worlds, you set yourself up for disappointment. (If I expect my special education students to outscore the advanced readers, I'm sure to fail. But if I can get my students to improve on their individual reading skills—and forget about the advanced readers altogether—then I will succeed and so will the students.) If your expertise is laying carpet, then don't compare yourself to a filmmaker or a chef. Aim to be the best carpet-layer, and forget about everybody else. Don't get your feelings hurt if the filmmaker gets an Oscar or the chef gets his own TV show. When they start giving out Oscars or TV shows for carpet-laying and you don't get one, that's when you can reasonably lament. Otherwise, just do your work, evaluating the quality each day to be sure it's the best that you can do. In this way, even if you are the person who cleans out the port-a-potties at the state fair, you can be successful.

1. Which would you rather have: private success or public success? Why? Give an example of each from your life.

2. In what ways do you reward yourself for a job well done?

3. If you had a chance to design your own trophy or plaque, what would it look like or say?

4. Think of someone from your community—perhaps someone from your book club, bunco club, or church group—who hasn't been recognized for a good deed or a giving spirit. Write that person a letter to let her know that you see and appreciate all that she does.

ON BEING GOOD ENOUGH

We're rarely satisfied with all that we are or all that we do. We lose twenty pounds, but now our face looks saggy. We mow the lawn so neatly, but the sidewalk still needs edging. Our hair is cut too short, or else it grows out too fast. We buy the perfect tablecloth, but against it, our napkins look dingy. Our jeans are too snug or baggy; our sweaters too blocky or slutty. Our Christmas tree, though pretty, could use a different topper. We run a mile, but wish for five. We run five miles, but it's not twenty-six. We whiten our teeth, but they're still crooked. We shop all day for the perfect gift and worry all night that we got it wrong.

1. Team up with a friend and develop a litany of your own dissatisfactions. Make it so ludicrous that you see how impossible your own expectations have become.

2. Do any patterns emerge? Are you more critical of yourself as a partner, as a mother, as a friend?

3. Who are the people you're trying to impress? How do you deal with judgment or criticism from outsiders?

4. In what ways might you slow yourself down so that instead of rushing to do and be more, you celebrate and champion what you already are? How can you become more generous with yourself?

Send participants away with additional challenges. Here are two I've used:

HOMEWORK ASSIGNMENTS

According to the Declaration of Independence, we Americans are entitled to life, liberty, and the pursuit of happiness. When you examine your own life, do you see any instances of being thwarted in attempts to procure these things? What specific things do you believe people are entitled to? What things do you think people should earn? Can you think of an occasion when you've been deprived of something you believe you're entitled to? Invite three friends to dinner and ask them to share with you their thoughts on entitlement. At the meal's end, order a dessert to share and observe who decides what you'll order, and how.

Find a time each day to empty yourself of you. Some people call this meditation; I call it damn hard work—but it's worth the effort. If you've read the Harry Potter books, you can picture Dumbledore and the stringy memories he pulls from his head and sets aside. Twirl your memories like spaghetti on a fork and get them out of your mind to make space for something bigger. If you're from a Christian tradition, you can think of what they call Centering Prayer, where you release all your thoughts and worries in order to be filled with God. Set the timer on your microwave for five or ten minutes, close your eyes, and take a deep breath. On the release, blow away all the youness. Let warm light take its place. When thoughts pop up, when your to-do list does a tap dance behind your eyes, picture it tapping right out the top of your head. Let it tap dance up to Jesus while you empty yourself again. Another breath, another try. It makes no difference how many times you have to send your thoughts and worries away. By choosing to empty again, by making yourself available again, you score.

CPSIA information can be obtained at www.ICGtesting.com
Printed in the USA
BVOW031139231212

308958BV00001B/2/P